"Tess, I..."

Zach began. His courage seemed to fail him.

Tess sat up straighter. "Yes?"

At last he made the words come. "I suppose you have a pretty good idea what this is about. It's a practical offer from a practical man. I need someone to keep the house and to keep me and the hands fed. Someone who knows the loneliness and plain day-to-day drudgery of life on a ranch." A ghost of a grin came and went on Zach's face. "And someone just crazy enough to want that kind of life for herself."

Zach looked up to her eyes. "Do you know what I'm getting at here, Tess?"

Her heart set up a terrible clatter. It sounded like thunder in her ears. She'd never imagined that she would be such a bundle of nerves about this. "I...I think so."

"Tess, I'm asking you to marry me."

Dear Reader,

With Mother's Day right around the corner, Special Edition commemorates the warm bonds of family. This month, parenthood brings some unlikely couples together in the most wondrous ways!

This May, Sherryl Woods continues her popular AND BABY MAKES THREE: THE NEXT GENERATION series. THAT SPECIAL WOMAN! Jenny Adams becomes an *Unexpected Mommy* when revenge-seeking single father Chance Adams storms into town and sweeps Jenny off her feet with his seductive charm!

Myrna Temte delivers book three of the MONTANA MAVERICKS: RETURN TO WHITEHORN series. In *A Father's Vow*, a hard-headed Native American hero must confront his true feelings for the vivacious schoolteacher who is about to give birth to his child. And look for reader favorite Lindsay McKenna's next installment in her mesmerizing COWBOYS OF THE SOUTHWEST series when a vulnerable heroine simply seeks solace on the home front, but finds her soul mate in a sexy *Stallion Tamer!*

Listen for wedding bells in *Practically Married* by Christine Rimmer. This final book in the CONVENIENTLY YOURS series is an irresistibly romantic tale about an arranged marriage between a cynical rancher and a soft-spoken single mom. Next, Andrea Edwards launches her DOUBLE WEDDING duet with *The Paternity Question*. This series features twin brothers who switch places and find love—and lots of trouble!

Finally, Diana Whitney caps off the month with *Baby in His Cradle*. In the concluding story of the STORK EXPRESS series, a *very* pregnant heroine desperately seeks shelter from the storm and winds up on the doorstep of a brooding recluse's mountain retreat.

I hope you treasure this book, and each and every story to come!

Sincerely,

Tara Gavin
Senior Editor & Editorial Coordinator

Please address questions and book requests to:
Silhouette Reader Service
U.S.: 3010 Walden Ave., P.O. Box 1325, Buffalo, NY 14269
Canadian: P.O. Box 609, Fort Erie, Ont. L2A 5X3

CHRISTINE RIMMER

PRACTICALLY MARRIED

Silhouette®

SPECIAL EDITION®

Published by Silhouette Books

America's Publisher of Contemporary Romance

To Arlene Evans, fellow writer from my Sacramento
RWA chapter and former school nurse, for seeing my
characters through any number of gunshot wounds,
sprains, contusions and broken bones. You're the
greatest, Arlene.

 SILHOUETTE BOOKS

ISBN 0-373-24174-7

PRACTICALLY MARRIED

Copyright © 1998 by Christine Rimmer

Books by Christine Rimmer

CHRISTINE RIMMER

came to her profession the long way around. Before settling down to write about the magic of romance, she'd been an actress, a sales clerk, a janitor, a model, a phone sales representative, a teacher, a waitress, a playwright and an office manager. Now that she's finally found work that suits her perfectly, she insists she never had a problem keeping a job—she was merely gaining "life experience" for her future as a novelist. Those who know her best withhold comment when she makes such claims; they are grateful that she's at last found steady work. Christine is grateful, too—not only for the joy she finds in writing, but for what waits when the day's work is through: a man she loves who loves her right back, and the privilege of watching their children grow and change day to day. She lives with her family in Oklahoma.

THE BRAVOS

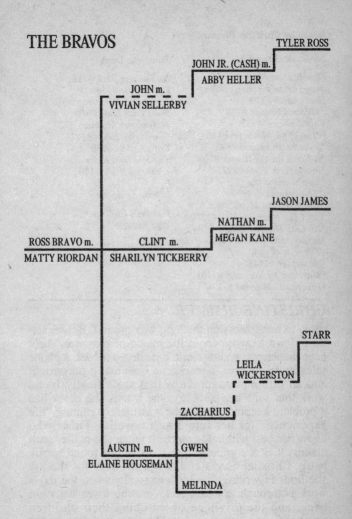

TYLER ROSS

JOHN JR. (CASH) m.
ABBY HELLER

JOHN m.
VIVIAN SELLERBY

JASON JAMES

NATHAN m.
MEGAN KANE

ROSS BRAVO m.   CLINT m.
MATTY RIORDAN   SHARILYN TICKBERRY

STARR

LEILA
WICKERSTON

ZACHARIUS

AUSTIN m.   GWEN
ELAINE HOUSEMAN

MELINDA

(Broken lines indicate previous marriages)

Chapter One

It was one-thirty in the afternoon on the last Sunday in April when Zach Bravo turned to Tess DeMarley and asked, "Will you go for a drive with me, Tess?"

Tess met his steady gray-blue eyes and knew immediately what would happen on that drive.

Ignoring the sudden acceleration of her heartbeat, she sat a little straighter and gave him a bright, direct smile. "Yes. I would enjoy a ride, Zach."

Edna Heller, with whom Tess lived, sat on the sofa a few feet away. Tess turned to the older woman. "Edna, would you mind if we left you on your own for a while?"

"Not at all. You two go on."

Tess thought of her daughter, Jobeth. After lunch, Jobeth had gone out to play with some neighbor kids. "Jobeth is off down the street at the Collerbys'. Do you think you could look after her while I'm gone?"

"Of course I will. Don't you worry about Jobeth. You two have yourselves a nice little ride."

Zach and Tess stopped in the small entry hall at the foot of the stairs to put on their coats. Then they went out together into the cold and windy afternoon.

When Zach opened the pickup door for her, Tess couldn't help noticing that he'd brought the best one, the newest one of the three he used out at the Rising Sun Ranch. It was a Chevy, a deep blue in color. And there wasn't a speck of mud or manure on it, inside or out. He must have washed it before he came to call.

That touched her, made silly tears push at the back of her throat. She swallowed them. She was not a woman who indulged in tears.

And there was no reason for tears anyway. Tess and Zach had spent a long, careful time with each other, slowly getting acquainted, each learning the other's ways and wants. And now Zach would make her an offer. It was nothing to cry over. It was a good and logical thing for all concerned.

As the pickup sped down the road, the wind whistled outside, blowing hard enough to make the cab shake. Tess stared through the windshield at the rolling prairie, the wide pale sky and the Big Horn Mountains in the distance, so tall and proud, silvery snow still thick on the tops of them and white clouds snagged on the crests. She had lived in Northeastern Wyoming for almost two years now. It was grand, harsh country; rich and green in early summer, cold and unforgiving in winter. More and more, she had begun to allow herself to think of it as home.

As they rode, Tess and Zach talked a little, about the newest addition to the Bravo family, Jason James, who'd been born just yesterday to Zach's cousin Nate and Nate's wife, Meggie. Zach had driven in to Buffalo, to the hospital there, to see the baby early that morning.

"Nate looked so proud," Zach said. "And I've never seen Meggie so happy. I think things between them have worked out, after all."

There had been some trouble between Nate and his wife. Tess was glad to hear the trouble was over. "That's good."

Zach chuckled. "Already that baby's got a set of lungs on him. You should hear him holler."

"I can't wait to get my hands on him." Tess thought of when Jobeth was a baby, of her tiny, perfect hands, her fat pink cheeks. Of the smell of her, that lovely, milky, baby-powder scent.

Zach took his gaze from the road long enough to turn his smile her way. He had a wonderful smile. All the Bravo men did.

A funny, weak feeling swept through Tess. Right then, for the first time, it became real to her that she might have more babies. With this man. It seemed an awfully intimate subject to consider—for a woman who would soon be made a strictly sensible offer.

Zach was looking at the road again. If Tess's face had turned red, he hadn't noticed—or else his natural tactfulness made him pretend that he hadn't.

A moment later, Zach slowed the pickup and turned onto a smaller road. A few minutes more, and the pavement wore out; the road turned to dirt. They bumped along, skirting ruts for a while.

Then Zach pulled to the shoulder next to a barbwire fence that stretched on in both directions as far as the eye could see.

Zach turned off the engine. In the quiet, the wind outside seemed to rise up louder and bump itself even harder against the truck. Zach gestured toward the snow-patched sweep of land beyond the fence. "This is Rising Sun land, as far as you can see."

The Rising Sun Cattle Company belonged to the Bravos, to Zach and Nate and their third cousin, Cash.

Cash. Tess thought the name, registered the inevitable ache it caused, and pushed it from her mind.

She smiled at the man behind the wheel. Of the three Bravo cousins who owned the Rising Sun, Zach was the one who lived there and worked the place full-time. A born rancher, everyone said of him. And from what Tess had seen in the past two years, everyone was right.

Zach pointed toward a stand of cottonwoods several hundred yards away. "Would you walk out there with me?"

Tess nodded, feeling formal and stiff—and a little bit scared. "Yes. Certainly."

They got out of the pickup. The wind, sharp and chill after the warmth of the cab, tore at Tess's jacket and tried to whip her hair out from under her wool hat. She hunched down into her jacket and stuck her gloved hands into her pockets.

Zach held the wires apart, so she could slide through the fence. She gave him a warm nod in thanks and eased through the space he'd made for her, taking care not to snag her clothes on the sharp barbs. Then, together but not touching, they slogged out to the bare cottonwoods, which clustered around a swiftly running stream—Crystal Creek, the stream was called, if Tess remembered right. It twisted and tumbled its way across a good portion of the Rising Sun Ranch.

"It's a pretty spot in summer," Zach said when they reached creekside. He sounded a little bewildered.

She hastened to let him know she found no fault with

the place he had chosen. "It's just fine, Zach." But in truth, it looked barren and drab, the ground half-frozen and muddy. The trees, still leafless this time of year, reminded her of weather-bleached bones.

Zach's strong shoulders lifted in a shrug. "It'll have to do."

She could hear the nervousness in his tone and knew just how he felt. Even though this was a practical matter, it was still a big step. She assured him once more, "It'll do just fine."

They shared a smile. The wind blew strands of her hair across her mouth. She caught them and eased them back under the edge of her hat.

He seemed to shake himself. "Here." Between them crouched a big, round boulder. He bent and brushed it off. "Sit down."

"Thank you." She perched on the boulder. It was an extremely cold seat; it made her bottom ache. But she didn't get up. It had been so thoughtful of him to offer it to her and to brush it off and all. Tess believed that thoughtfulness should always be appreciated.

Zach coughed. "Tess, I..." His courage seemed to fail him.

She sat up straighter, willing him to be able to go on. "Yes?"

He coughed again, into his gloved fist. Then, at last, he made the words come. "I suppose you have a pretty good idea what this is about. It's a practical offer from a practical man. I need someone to keep the house and to keep me and the hands fed. Someone who knows the loneliness and plain day-to-day drudgery of life on a ranch." A ghost of a grin came and went on his face. "And someone just crazy enough to want that kind of life for herself."

She stared at him, thinking of the South Dakota ranch

that had been her childhood home. Zach was right. It hadn't been an easy life. But it had been a life she'd loved, a life she'd only left to follow her husband. She had believed at the time that she could always go back.

Oh, what a foolish girl she had been.

Zach hitched a booted foot up on the side of the boulder where she sat, looked down at the frozen ground by his other boot—and then up into her eyes. "Do you know what I'm getting at here, Tess?"

Her heart had set up a terrible clatter. It sounded like thunder in her ears. She'd never imagined that she would be such a bundle of nerves about this. "I...I think so."

He took his boot off the boulder, slid his hat off his head and rolled the brim nervously in his two hands. "Tess, I'm asking you to marry me."

In spite of the gentle way he said those words, they came at her stronger and sharper than the Wyoming wind. She found she couldn't sit still, so she shot to her feet, walked in a circle, and then sat back down. "I see."

He frowned, fiddled with his hat brim a little more, then stuck the hat back on his head. "I thought you knew. I thought marriage was where we were headed."

"Well, yes. I...I did know. And we've talked of marriage, of what we both wanted from marriage, haven't we? Often."

"But you seem surprised."

She gulped. "No, really. I'm not."

"Tess. You should see your face."

She blinked, shook her head. "No, I'm not surprised. I mean, I *am* surprised, but not about you proposing. I mean... Oh, I don't know...." She made herself stop babbling, took a moment to breathe deeply, to try to find some shred of composure somewhere in her agitated mind and heart.

Silently, as she breathed carefully in and out, she reminded herself of what mattered: that Zach Bravo offered her the life she longed for. That she liked Zach. And that the two of them sought the same things. They were both honorable people who would work hard to build a good future together. Zach Bravo would make a fine husband. He was a man who would always take care of his own, a man she would be able to count on.

And to a widowed single mother with minimal wage-earning skills, a man she could count on sounded pretty darn good.

Still…

"Tess?"

She closed her eyes. "Just…give me a minute, okay?"

"All right."

She rose again from the freezing rock, and turned away from Zach, to look westward toward the rugged peaks of the mountains. Somewhere behind her, from the other side of the creek, faintly, she heard a mournful cry, as of a dove, a sad, cooing sound.

And she couldn't stop herself; she saw Cash's face. She saw him grinning that warm, teasing grin of his.

Her heart seemed to get small and tight inside her chest. He was so splendid: golden-haired, blue-eyed Cash. Zach's cousin. And the one who had always come through for her and Jobeth when all hope was gone.

Cash had been her dead husband's buddy since high school. And Cash Bravo never deserted a friend.

Tess could almost feel the touch of his hand now, pressing money she hated to take but couldn't afford to refuse into her palm. Over and over, though he must have known he was only throwing good money after bad, he had bankrolled her husband's crazy wildcatting schemes. All it ever took was a phone call—and Cash would come.

When Josh died, Cash was there to help her through the funeral. And to offer her and Jobeth a new start, in Medicine Creek, living with Edna, who had been ill at the time and needed someone to care for her.

Cash was her friend and her hero. And she loved him with all of her heart.

Tess held her face up to the biting wind and closed her eyes again, tightly, as she ticked off the hard facts.

Cash Bravo was happily married and deeply in love with his wife, Abby—who was Edna's daughter, and who considered Tess her friend. Cash had no idea of Tess's feelings for him—and he never would. It was her guilty secret, a secret she would carry to her grave.

A secret that would never hurt Zach. Because Zach wasn't asking for her heart. He'd made that clear from the first. Zach wanted a loyal wife and a life's partner, a suitable mother for any children they might have. Tess could be those things for him. There was no reason he would ever have to know of the hidden, pointless yearnings of her stubborn heart.

From somewhere within the wind that blew around her, Tess could almost hear a sad voice chiding, *If he's to be your husband, he deserves the truth.*

Tess ignored the voice. She would tell no one of her love for Cash. No one. Ever.

"Tess?"

She turned back to Zach and gave him a wobbly smile.

He asked, "Are you worried about Jobeth?"

Her smile grew brighter. The answer to that question was easy. "I'm not worried in the least. Jobeth is crazy about you."

Strangely Jobeth was enough like Zach that she could have been his natural daughter. She had light brown hair like his, and eyes of a similar shade. But more than looks, she had a temperament like Zach's: even and serious, cautious in a touching and tender way. Jobeth had always looked at her own father with wariness. She'd shied away from Josh's loud voice and pulled into herself when he grabbed her for a hug. Yet she reached out to Zach, she followed him around. She lived for visits to the ranch, where she loved nothing more than to go out with Zach in the morning and come home at noon, grinning and covered with mud, to announce proudly that she'd helped pull a calf from a ditch or been chased by a bad-tempered bull.

"She's a fine girl," Zach said. "Marry me, and I will treat her as my own—if she'll let me."

Tess wrinkled her nose at him. "She'll let you. And you know she will." An extra hard gust of wind hit her, cutting right through her heavy jacket like an icy knife. Tess wrapped her arms around herself and shivered.

Zach watched her shiver and felt like a fool for dragging her out here. It had seemed the right thing, the fitting thing to do: to bring her out on the land to make his proposal. But now they were here, he could see that a warm living room with a cheery fire blazing in the grate would have been a wiser choice.

She cupped her gloved hands over her red nose and blew on them, warming her face a bit with her own breath. The harsh wind pulled wisps of her curly dark hair from under her hat and blew them wildly around her face.

Zach wanted to reach out and put his arms around her, to protect her from the cold. But he restrained the urge to shield her with his body. That was something a lover would do.

And love was not the issue here. They both knew that. They'd discussed what they each wanted from a life's partner often and at length.

Both of them had married once for what they had thought was love; and both were determined they wouldn't make that mistake the second time around.

This time, Zach had chosen a woman purely for compatibility. Tess had been born to ranching people and she loved the ranching life. He'd learned the hard way that a woman's love of his chosen life mattered a lot more than any passion she might feel toward him.

There was one more subject to tackle before he asked for her answer. "We should probably talk about Starr, too."

Tess nodded and dropped her hands away from her face. "Oh, yes. Your daughter. She's…?"

"Sixteen," he supplied flatly, wanting to get the information out, to get this talk of his lost, messed-up child behind them. "She lives in San Diego, with her mother. She used to come and stay with me in the summertime. But the past few years…" He didn't know how to finish, so he just shook his head.

Sympathy and understanding made Tess's fine dark eyes look even softer than usual. "I'm sorry."

Zach took off his hat again, hit it against his thigh and then eased it back on once more. "It's how it goes sometimes. Over the years, with the distance between us and the…hostility between her mother and me, well, somehow I lost Starr. She's like a stranger to me now. But I just wanted to be sure you understood that she's still my responsibility. I send her mother regular support checks. And it's always possible she could turn up one of these days. If that happened…"

Tess finished his sentence for him, with much more assurance than he could have mustered. "…we would welcome her, for a visit, or to live with us, whichever it turned out to be. And I sincerely hope to meet her soon."

Zach quelled the urge to mutter, Not damn likely and you'd be sorry if you did. Instead he asked the big question, directly this time. "Will you have me as your husband, Tess?"

After a long and agonizing silence, she gave him the words he sought.

"Yes, Zach. I will."

Chapter Two

During the drive back to Medicine Creek Tess asked, "What about Angie?"

Zach shot her a quick look. "Didn't I tell you? She's leaving a week from Monday. Going to live with a daughter in Denver."

Angie Iberlin was Zach's current cook and housekeeper, the latest in a long line of them in the past couple of years. For over two decades, Edna had handled the job. But her illness had forced her to quit and she'd decided not to return. Zach hadn't had much luck in trying to replace her.

Tess hid a smile. Now she understood what had finally pushed Zach into popping the question. He would rather take a chance on marriage again than to try to find another housekeeper. That was okay with Tess. She didn't care what had inspired him to take the big step. He had done it; that was good enough.

When they got to the house, they found Edna waiting for them.

"Did you have a nice ride? *Brr.* It's so cold out today. Come in, come in." She took their coats and hats and gloves and hung them on the rack by the door, then she herded them into the kitchen. "Coffee?"

Tess took the older woman by the shoulders and aimed her at the table. "Sit down. I'll get it."

"It's made. Fresh. I knew that when you came home, you'd probably want—"

Zach laughed. "Edna, sit down."

Edna dropped to the chair and looked from Zach to Tess and back again. "I...I had the strangest feeling, while you were gone. I thought that maybe..." Her voice trailed off on an expectant note.

Tess got the cups from the cupboard and the little cream pitcher, too. "You thought that maybe *what?*"

"Oh, you know. I know you know."

Zach laughed. "You know we know *what?*"

Edna pursed her mouth. "Zacharius Bravo, don't tease me. You know I hate to be teased."

Zach gave in. "All right. The truth is, I proposed."

Edna let out a glad cry. "I knew it. I knew it." She turned to look at Tess. "And?"

Tess filled the cream pitcher. "I accepted."

Edna put her hand to her heart. "Oh. I can hardly believe it. When? When will it be?"

With Angie leaving, Tess knew Zach would want the wedding soon. She shot him a questioning look.

"This coming Saturday?" he suggested. "At the county courthouse?"

"Sounds fine with me."

"And we'll have a party after," Edna announced. "Out at the ranch. Oh, there's so much to do...."

Jobeth came in a few minutes later. At the sight of Zach, her face lit up. "You're still here. Are we going out to the ranch?"

Tess answered for Zach. "Not today." She watched the excitement fade from Jobeth's eyes. "But sit down. We want to talk to you."

As soon as she heard the news, Jobeth was beaming again. "We'll live at the ranch, won't we? Forever and ever. When can we move in, Zach? When can we go?"

"Right after the wedding. How's that?"

With shining eyes, Jobeth declared that right after the wedding would be just fine with her.

Tess worked full-time at a gift shop, Amestoy's Treasure Trove, over on Main Street. First thing Monday, Tess told her employer, Carmen Amestoy, that she was marrying Zach Bravo and that Friday would be her last day.

Carmen threw up her plump hands and exclaimed, "Oh, no! How will I get along without you?" And then she went on, in that way she had of never waiting for the answer to a question. "Well, it's not exactly tourist season yet. And things have been slow as molasses in January flowing uphill. So I guess I'll manage somehow. And it's about time Zach Bravo proposed. I want you to be happy. You will be, won't you? And please don't be a stranger. All the customers will miss you. Am I invited to the wedding? Well, of course, I am."

"Carmen, we're only going to the courthouse, over in Buffalo."

"The party after, then. I'll come to that. It'll be at Cash and Abby's, am I right?"

Tess shook her head. "Well, no. It'll be—"

"If not at Cash and Abby's, then out at the Rising Sun."

"Yes. At the ranch. But it's only going to be a small—"

"Whatever. I'll come."

"Of course, if you'd like to."

"I suppose you'll want to shorten your hours a little, for the rest of the week, in order to get everything ready."

"As a matter of fact—"

"All right, all right. Consider yourself part-time."

"Thanks."

"Now, where are you going for your honeymoon? I think, this time of year, someplace tropical would be—"

"We're not."

"*What?* That's insane. Zach Bravo's got plenty of money. He can certainly afford to leave his precious cows for a week or two and take his new bride someplace she'll always remember."

"Carmen, we can't spare the time to go on any honeymoon."

Carmen looked crestfallen. "But...you're newlyweds."

"We have a ranch to run."

The older woman muttered something about ranchers and the total lack of romance in their souls. Then she spoke briskly, "All right, all right. If you don't want a honeymoon, that's your business. Who am I to tell you how to run your life? Who am I to point out that a man and a woman should have a little time, just for the two of them, when they first start out? I'm only Carmen. Your boss, part-time, until Friday..."

"Oh, Carmen..."

"No, no. It's all right. It *is* your life, after all. What will you wear to be married in? I know. You'll wear the dress you love. Come right this way."

Carmen kept a small clothing section in the rear of the shop. She led Tess there and made her try on the lavender silk dress with the peplum waist that Tess had been coveting from the day it came in.

"I know you love it," Carmen said. "And I know you couldn't afford it. But now you don't have to. Because I'm giving it to you. As a wedding present."

"Oh, no, Carmen, I couldn't—"

"Don't argue with me. I'm your boss. Until Friday, anyway. That dress was made for you. No one else will have it. And you will not pay a cent for it. Now here, try it on...."

Tess tried to keep saying no, but Carmen was determined and Tess did want the dress. In the end, she accepted the gift—and spent money she shouldn't have spent on a satiny nightgown and lacy negligee in almost the same shade as the dress.

"Just be happy," Carmen sniffed. "That's all I ask. Now, don't stand around. Check that shipment of hurricane lamps. See that none of them are broken. Can you do that? Of course you can. You're a gem and I don't know how I'll get along without you...."

Tess spent Monday and Tuesday nights packing up for the move. She and Jobeth didn't have a lot, but still, getting everything ready to go took time.

On Wednesday, Jobeth turned eight. They had talked the week before about inviting a few of her school friends over for cake and party games. But with all the excitement about the wedding, Tess had dropped the ball. The party just wasn't going to happen.

"I'm so sorry, honey," she told Jobeth that morning.

Jobeth looked puzzled. "Why be sorry? Zach's coming tonight, with a stock trailer to move our stuff, isn't he?"

"Yes. And instead of celebrating your special day, we'll be moving our things."

"But, Mom, we'll go out to the ranch! I'll see Tick and Tack. And Bozo." Tick and Tack were her favorite barn cats. And Bozo was a bum calf, orphaned during a big blizzard a few weeks before, a calf that Jobeth already thought of as her own. "*That's* the way to spend a birthday, if you ask me."

"Well," Tess said indulgently. "I'm glad you're not *too* disappointed."

"Mom. How could I be disappointed? We're going to the *ranch.*" And with that, she slung her pack onto her shoulder and headed out for school.

Zach arrived with the stock trailer, as promised, at a little after four. They had everything loaded within an hour. Naturally Jobeth begged to ride with Zach. So Tess followed behind them in her ancient 4X4 Tercel. She had a gift for Jobeth on the seat beside her. She planned to present it to her daughter during dinner—which she had prepared herself and put in plastic containers, all ready to heat and serve. Angie Iberlin, Zach's soon-to-be-ex-housekeeper, was a neat and polite person. She kept things tidy. But her cooking left a lot to be desired. With Tess bringing the meal, she could be sure they would eat well. Earlier that afternoon, she'd called Angie and told her not to worry about fixing dinner for them.

When they pulled into the yard at the ranch, Tess looked out the windshield at the two-story ranch house and just couldn't help feeling a little proprietary. The wood siding on the house had been painted a soft dove gray. Tess liked the color, but had noticed during other visits that the paint had started to fade and peel in a few places. She would have to do something about that—after the weather warmed, of course, after she got her garden going and whipped the interior of the house into reasonable shape.

Zach pulled the trailer around back. Tess followed where he led.

They found the house empty, as expected. By now, Angie would have gone on over to the foreman's cottage across the yard, where she stayed when she wasn't engaged in her housekeeping duties. The three cowhands who worked alongside Zach lived in individual house trailers not far from Angie's cottage. Angie would serve them their meals in the trailers.

By six, the stock trailer was empty. Tess's things waited in the big master bedroom. And Jobeth had carried hers to the room Zach had chosen for her. Zach began lugging the rest—a few pieces of furniture and some kitchen equipment—down to the big basement, where Tess could deal with it later.

In the master suite, Tess discovered that Zach had cleared out one side of the walk-in closet. Half of the huge double bureau was likewise empty, ready for Tess's clothes. As she hung her new nightgown and negligee in the closet, Tess couldn't help thinking that in just a few days, she and Zach would be sharing more than a closet and a bureau in that room. She blushed at the thought, and felt grateful that no one was there to see.

It would be awkward, she was certain, to make love when they didn't have that kind of feeling for each other. But she wanted more children so very much. She had always wanted more little ones to raise, though she'd taken great care never to get pregnant again during her marriage to Josh. They'd had too much trouble getting by as it was.

But now, with Zach, things would be different. Zach knew how she felt about children and he had agreed that having more would be fine with him. So after they married on Saturday, they would sleep together, in the big four-poster bed with its pineapple finials. And if God was kind, soon enough there would be a new Bravo baby for Tess to love.

Tess hung her few good dresses on hangers and filled three of the bureau drawers. The rest of her wardrobe she left in boxes, which she pushed into the closet on the side Zach had cleared for her. She would put it all away properly after the wedding.

She had just gathered up the empty boxes to carry downstairs when she thought she heard a car pull up out in the yard. The big windows of the master bedroom faced the front of the house, so she drew back the curtain and looked out. Down below, Cash's Cadillac gleamed in the gathering twilight.

Tess's heart leapt in guilty joy at the thought of seeing him—of sharing a few friendly words, of watching him smile. Dropping the empty boxes to worry about later, she flew to the mirror over the bureau and smoothed her hair. Then she hurried from the room.

She found Edna waiting at the foot of the stairs, holding a layer cake on a silver plate. Tess could make out the words, Much Happiness—Tess and Zach written in blue icing on top.

"Surprise!" Edna exclaimed. Then she grinned. "We're here to make a party. An engagement and birthday party. We've brought food. And two cakes. One for the birthday girl. And this one—" she lifted the cake she held higher "— for you and Zach."

"But…I brought our dinner," Tess explained idiotically.

Cash, who stood a few feet behind Edna, laughed his deep laugh and held out the second cake. "The more food the better, especially if you cooked it, Tess."

Thrilled at the sight of him, warmed by the sound of

his voice, Tess beamed at him in pure adoration—but only for an instant. She quickly caught herself. She blinked and looked away—and right into Zach's eyes as he came up the basement stairs across from where she stood.

Tess's stomach lurched. For a second that seemed to stretch on into forever, time stopped.

Tess thought, He knows. He saw. It's all over now.

Then Zach asked in a perfectly normal tone of voice, "What's going on?"

"A party," Tess said faintly. She forced a light laugh. "They're giving us a party."

Just then, they heard voices in the front hall.

"That will be Nate and Meggie," Edna said.

"And the baby?" Tess asked, always excited at the prospect of a little one to hold—and right then eager to focus on anything else but what Zach might or might not have seen. "Are they bringing the baby?"

Edna nodded. "Let's go have a look at him. And then we must help Abigail. She's bringing in the rest of the food."

Ten minutes later, Edna had commandeered the formal dining room and bidden Angie to come back across the yard and help her with the table. The men and Jobeth had wandered out to the barn to have a look at a Black Angus bull that Zach had just bought. The younger women, Meggie, Abby and Tess, had moved into the great room with the new baby and Abby's toddler, Tyler Ross.

Meggie and Abby sat on the big sofa. Tess sat across from the Bravo wives in an easy chair, with tiny Jason James cradled in her arms. Tyler Ross, standing on his own two pudgy legs, clutched the side of her chair and gazed up at her through eyes as blue as his father's.

"Bay-bee," Tyler Ross said with great care.

"Yes," Tess replied dreamily, reveling in the sweet,

warm weight of the bundle in her arms. "Baby. A big, handsome, incredible baby boy."

Over on the couch, Abby chuckled.

Tess looked up and caught the other two women sharing a glance. "What?" she demanded.

Abby brushed a hank of blond hair out of her eyes and spoke with affection. "It's just you. You're such a... *woman*. Put a baby in your arms and give you a menu to plan and you're in hog heaven."

Tess pursed her mouth. "And this is bad?"

Meggie, who had circles under her eyes as a testament to new motherhood—and a soft smile on her face as proof that things really were going well with Nate—spoke up. "No, it's not bad. It's terrific. *You're* terrific. And we're so relieved Zach has finally snapped you up."

"I'll second that." Abby laughed. "Though of course, I knew from the first that you and Zach were meant for each other."

Tess tried not to think of blond hair and sky blue eyes. "You did?"

Abby nodded, looking smug. "On my wedding night, after all the guests went home and Cash and I were finally alone, I predicted that Nate would marry Meggie. And that Zach would get hitched up with you. Cash said I was nuts, that Zach would never marry again and Nate would never marry at all. But who'll have the last laugh here?"

Tess smiled and gently rocked the baby in her arms. "You, Abby. Definitely you."

Abby pushed her hair out of her eyes again. "You bet I will."

Tess went on smiling. She cared deeply for Abby. And she knew that Abby cared for her. Over the past two years, since Tess had come to Medicine Creek, they'd been through some scary times together. And when Abby and

Cash had hit a rocky patch in their marriage, Tess had gone right to Abby and urged her to work things out. For Tess, there had been no thought of doing otherwise. She had known from the first time she saw them together that Abby and Cash were born to be man and wife.

Abby leaned forward on the couch. "What is going through that mind of yours?"

Tess only kept smiling and rocking the baby. "Nothing. Nothing at all."

Right then, Edna appeared in the door to the hall that led to the kitchen. "Tess, there is simply too much food. I'm going to have to put what you brought in the refrigerator. Angie can heat it up for tomorrow. Is that all right?"

"That's fine."

Edna looked at her daughter. "Angie and I could use a little help around here."

Tess shifted the precious bundle in her arms. "Let me—"

"No," Edna said firmly. "You will sit there in that chair and relax for once. You're always waiting on us. Tonight, it's our turn."

Abby laughed. "As much as I hate to agree with my mother, she's right. Stay there. I think I can manage to put the food into serving bowls and carry the bowls to the table."

"Just as long as you don't actually have to *cook* anything," Tess teased. Abby had little skill in the kitchen— and was darn proud of it.

"Don't worry," Abby promised. "If she tries to make me do anything resembling actual food preparation, I'll run out the back door—for everybody's sake."

"Come on, Abigail, don't dawdle," said Edna, turning back toward the kitchen and the food waiting there.

Alone with the little ones, Meggie and Tess talked mostly of mundane things, of the weather, which should be warming to true spring very soon, and of Tess's various plans for getting the house in order.

At one point, Tess couldn't resist remarking softly, "It's good to see you and Nate looking so happy."

Meggie colored a little. "He's the only one I've ever loved. And he's finally realized he loves me, too." She reached for her nephew, Tyler Ross, who had toddled over to drool on her leg. He went into her arms and she pulled him up to perch on her lap.

"You'll be working the Double-K together, I take it?" Tess asked. The Double-K was Meggie's ranch.

"Yes," Meggie said. Tyler Ross had started squirming. She set him on the floor and handed him a rubber ring to chew on. "We'll be working together." She looked up and met Tess's eyes. "From now on." Her tired face seemed to glow with pure happiness.

Tess felt glad for her. And just a little bit jealous, too. Meggie and Nate were like Abby and Cash: a man and a woman perfectly suited to each other, who also happened to be deeply and passionately in love.

Tess knew that she and Zach were well suited. But as for the rest...

Well suited is fine, she told herself firmly. Well suited is a lot more than you ever dared to hope you would get.

She was no longer some dreamy-eyed teenager. She knew now that the world could be a cruel, unforgiving place, that a person had to work hard—and grab her chance when it came.

She also knew that passionate love was a luxury, one that rarely came in the same package with a good and dependable man. A fortunate few, like Abby and Meggie, might find everything rolled into one. But for people like

Tess, a productive life and a solid partnership would just have to do.

Right then, Abby appeared from the central hall. "Somebody go get the men and Jobeth. They have to wash up. My mother, the drill sergeant, says we're sitting down to dinner in ten minutes."

"I'll go." Tess rose from the chair and gave the baby to Meggie.

Outside, it was a clear night with only a mild wind. Tess left the house through the rear door off the enclosed back porch, and started across the backyard to the barn and sheds. But the night beguiled her. For a moment, she paused and looked up at the pale stars that would grow brighter as the night deepened. The air smelled sweet, of new grass with just a hint of cedar blown down from the distant mountains. Oh, yes, it was spring, all right.

She heard a sound, and turned to find that little black-baldy calf, Bozo, ambling toward her. He came right up to her and nuzzled her fingers.

"Sorry, boy. No milk here," she told him.

The little bum figured it out himself after a few seconds, and trotted off on his spindly legs. She smiled, watching him, thinking that she'd have to insist he stayed fenced once she got going on her garden. He was a bandit already; she could tell by the way he'd tried to suck from her fingers, a survivor who would steal milk from any cow who stood still long enough. Tess respected survivors; she considered herself one. But Bozo wouldn't get a chance to devour the tender leaves of her bedding plants if she had anything to say about it.

She started toward the outbuildings again, but she didn't get more than a step or two before the men appeared around the side of one of the sheds. They saw her standing there and they stopped for a moment, three tall, proud figures against the night.

They moved toward her with their long strides again. As they approached, Zach asked, "What is it, Tess?"

Through the darkness, Tess tried to read the secrets behind his eyes. What did you see? she wondered silently. And what did it mean to you? But his eyes gave nothing away.

Over the months they'd been seeing each other, she had thought that she'd grown to know him. Yet right then she felt as if she didn't know him at all. He was the stranger who would soon be her husband.

"Tess?" He was frowning at her.

She realized she hadn't answered his question. "Dinnertime. Where's Jobeth?"

He turned and called for her daughter. Jobeth appeared immediately, sliding out from between the big doors of the barn. "I'm here, Zach."

"You let Bozo out," he told her in that kind, careful voice of his. "Better get him back behind a fence."

"I will, Zach. Right away."

"And then come in and wash up. It's time for dinner."

"Okay." The child hurried after the calf.

Tess sighed when she looked at what Edna had wrought, at the ivory lace tablecloth, the gleaming china and silver, the snowy linen napkins, all set off so perfectly by the soft glow of candlelight. "Oh, Edna, it's beautiful."

Edna went to one end of the table and pulled out the chair there. With great formality, she instructed, "You will sit here." She gestured at the other end. "And Zacharius will sit there."

Tess remained standing. Edna always took the hostess's

seat at any formal meal. Tess knew how much that seat meant to her. "Oh, Edna. No…"

Edna pulled the chair out farther. "I mean it. You sit down. You sit down right here."

Tess obeyed, sliding into the seat of honor. She felt Edna's slim hand touch her shoulder lightly and she reached back long enough to give that hand a quick squeeze. Then she busied herself with sliding the silver filigree ring from her napkin and smoothing the napkin across her lap.

When she looked up, she found Zach watching her from down the table. She thought of that moment on the stairs and her heart kind of froze for an instant, then commenced beating too fast. He smiled. She smiled back, praying that she looked more composed than she felt, wondering if his smile was a *real* smile, thinking that his eyes looked a little bit cold.

She picked up her water glass and drank from it. As she set the glass down, she told herself to quit worrying. It must be okay, with Zach. If he had seen anything in that look she'd given Cash, he wouldn't be smiling at her.

Would he?

Abby appeared then, bearing a huge rack of lamb. Everyone *oohed* and *ahhed* over it.

"Don't worry," she assured them all, laughing. "I didn't cook it. It'll taste just as good as it looks."

It turned out that Abby's housekeeper, Mrs. Helm, had prepared the feast. Everyone agreed that it was *almost* as good as something Tess might have done.

Cash had provided several bottles of excellent wine. The toasting went on long after most of the food had been eaten. Through the meal, Tess took great care never to look too long in Cash's direction. And when she thought Zach didn't notice, she watched him a lot. By the time dessert was served, she had succeeded in convincing herself that Zach had noticed nothing. Everything was just as it had always been. Her secret remained hers alone.

As Edna carried Jobeth's cake to the table, Cash produced a pile of presents to go with the one Tess had brought. Tess felt the usual flush of adoring thankfulness toward him. He was so generous, so thoughtful, so kind.

But this time, she kept her guard up. Her expression remained composed and her smile was no more than appropriately grateful.

Jobeth made a wish and blew out her candles. Then she opened her gifts.

Next came the engagement cake. And more toasts. It was near nine before Meggie and Nate insisted they just had to go. Everyone trooped outside to say goodbye. Then Edna kept Cash and Abby there an extra half hour, getting the plates scraped and stacked so that Angie wouldn't have too big a job the next morning.

Finally Tess and Zach stood together on the porch, waving, as Cash and his family piled into the Cadillac.

As soon as the big car drove away, Tess turned to Zach. "It's almost ten. We should get going, too."

He said nothing.

She pulled her sweater closer around her and folded her arms across her waist. "Zach?" Her pulse picked up, as the guilt and worry she'd managed to push to the deeper recesses of her mind came popping to the surface once again. "Is something wrong?" The dangerous question escaped her of its own accord.

Zach's brows drew together. Hardly daring to breathe, cursing herself for a thousand kinds of fool for asking a question to which an answer would most likely bring disaster, Tess waited for him to speak.

But he didn't speak. Instead, very gently, he put out a hand.

Wary, not knowing what he meant to do, she almost jerked back.

But then she stopped herself. He would be her husband. She shouldn't shy away from his touch.

His hand slid under her hair, to wrap around her nape. His skin felt rough—and warm. She gasped a little, in surprise. It was crazy, but now she thought about it, she couldn't remember ever having felt his touch before.

Was that possible? They would marry in three days— yet this was the first time he had laid a hand on her. How could that be so?

Really, he must have taken her arm now and then, grasped her hand in greeting or in aid.

Yet she could not remember any of those casual contacts. Surely they had occurred. So why couldn't she recall a one of them?

Somewhere out in the night, an owl asked, "Who? Who?"

Tess started to turn her head toward the sound.

"No. Don't," Zach whispered softly.

She blinked and met his unreadable eyes, trying to appear calm and relaxed, praying that he couldn't hear the rapid pounding of her heart.

His rough thumb moved. It caressed the pulse point at the side of her throat.

And she realized that whether he heard it or not, he did know. Oh, yes. He knew how fast her heart raced. He could feel it, right under his hand.

Gently, relentlessly, he pulled her closer. She didn't fully believe that he would kiss her until his lips met hers.

Chapter Three

At first, Tess kept her arms wrapped protectively around herself, so that her body hardly touched Zach's.

But the distance she maintained didn't seem to bother him. He kissed her sweetly. Slowly. Tenderly. He didn't try to pull her closer.

Tess closed her eyes. She found she liked the scent of him, a healthy scent of soap and clean skin and leather. He tasted faintly of coffee, which Edna had served with dessert. After a moment, she stopped clutching her middle and dared to reach up, to put her hands on his shoulders. They were lean and hard under her fingers, the shoulders of a man who used his body in his work.

He let go of her nape and slid both hands to her waist, grasping firmly, stepping a fraction closer, brushing himself against her, but just barely. It felt nice. It felt as if his body was kind of whispering to hers.

She heard herself sigh.

And then he lifted his head and put her carefully away from him.

She let her eyelids flutter open. The night seemed so still. In the light of the porch lamp, she could see him quite clearly. She stared up at his craggy, serious face— and couldn't think of a thing to say.

She felt stunned. As tender as the kiss had been, there was no mistaking its intent. It was a kiss a man gives a woman. The kind of kiss Tess had only shared with one other man in her life—her husband, Josh.

Hardly knowing she would do it, she reached up and touched her lips. It seemed she could still feel the kiss there, so warm and sweet. So full of the promise of what was to come.

He smiled, just a little.

And she smiled back. She was glad he had kissed her, glad to learn that she could enjoy kissing him. Maybe when they got to the big bed with the pineapple finials, it wouldn't be so terribly difficult, after all.

"Come on," he said, taking her hand.

They went back inside to find Jobeth snoozing on the sofa in the great room.

Tess perched beside her and tenderly stroked the brown hair back from her forehead. "Honey, wake up. Time to go home."

Mumbling and groaning, Jobeth sat up and stretched. "Oh. Do we *have* to?"

Tess nodded. "Yes, we do. And right now."

A few minutes later, Zach stood in the back driveway watching the taillights of Tess's battered little car as it disappeared around the front, headed for the gate and the highway beyond. He heard the car's tired engine revving as Tess turned onto the road. Moments later, the sound had faded to nothing.

He was alone with the night.

He started for the house, but then a nighthawk called from somewhere nearby. Turning that way, he saw the shadowy outline of the bird as it dived through the dark after some luckless insect.

Zach changed his mind about going in. Right then he would feel trapped in the house. He turned and headed for the horse pasture instead.

At the split-rail fence, he whistled. Ladybird, his favorite mare, came trotting over.

He stroked the blaze on her forehead and blew in her nostrils. "Sorry, sweetheart," he whispered, when she nuzzled his palm. "No carrots tonight."

She gave him a little snort and allowed a few more strokes before she turned and took off. Leaning on the fence, he watched her go, then ended up staring off blindly across the dark pasture toward the mountains and the quarter moon that hung low in the sky.

He kept thinking of Tess. Picturing her face, remembering her expression just after he'd kissed her. She'd looked so sweet and pretty and surprised, putting her hand to her mouth, as if his kiss still lingered there.

She had liked that kiss. And her expression had told him as clearly as any words that she hadn't expected to like it.

Probably, he shouldn't have kissed her. Not tonight, anyway.

Maybe not ever...

Zach turned and braced the heel of a boot on the bottom rail of the fence. He stared at the house his grandfather had built and tried to get used to what he'd probably suspected all along, but knew for certain as of tonight.

He had seen the look she'd given Cash. And now he had to face the truth: Like nearly every other female for miles around, his wife-to-be was totally gone on his big-spending, blue-eyed cousin.

Zach tipped his head back toward the sky and looked at the stars as thick and shiny as glitter-glue overhead. He knew damn well that, whatever Tess felt, nothing would come of it. Cash belonged to Abby, heart and soul. And, anyway, Zach had learned a lot about Tess in the months it had taken him to ask her to be his wife. He knew, with no doubt whatsoever, that she wasn't the kind who would let herself get too close to another woman's man, no matter what she felt for that man.

Ladybird wandered back over. She let out a playful snort and nudged Zach in the shoulder. He turned around and petted her some more, whispering to her softly, thinking that, from a practical standpoint, Tess DeMarley was exactly the wife he wanted. He'd look the rest of his life before he found another who suited his needs so well. And Jobeth. That kid was something. He wanted the chance to raise her to be the rancher she was meant to be.

Zach gave his horse a final pat and turned for the house.

He just had to *stay* practical about this, that was all. He didn't have to go and make a big deal out of some *feeling* that Tess was never going to act on, anyway. Maybe, in time, what she felt for Cash would fade by itself. Meanwhile, she could keep her little secret, and they could still have a good life.

They just had to take time. Take it slow.

Yes, she did appeal to him as a woman.

But he wasn't some breeding bull driven by urges he couldn't control. He'd been a virgin when he married his ex-wife, Leila, and except for that tough time right after she walked out on him, when he was looking for any way to dull the pain she'd left behind, he'd kept his equipment inside his pants. Unlike Cash, who'd been a real ladies' man, and Nate, who'd been just plain wild, Zach's sexual experience was pretty limited. He supposed he was old-fashioned. He felt that there were some things a man only ought to do with his wife. And that those things should not be taken lightly.

Zach's dog, Reggie, was waiting by the back door for him. Zach bent long enough to give him a scratch behind the ear and then went ahead and let him in to sleep on the back porch.

By the time he headed up the stairs, he knew what he would do. He would marry Tess on Saturday, just as they'd planned. And then he would give them both a little time to discover how close they really wanted their marriage to be.

"Great food, good music and fine company," Carmen Amestoy told Tess that Saturday evening, three hours after Tess and Zach had exchanged their wedding vows. The older woman talked with her usual animation as she balanced an overflowing plate on her plump knees. "Did you change your mind and decide to go on a honeymoon after all? Never mind, forget it. I can see by your face that you didn't." She popped an olive into her mouth and gave Tess's sleeve a pat. "You look lovely, honey. A beautiful bride—for the second time around. The dress is just right. Are you happy? I know you are. My loss is Zach's gain...."

Angie Iberlin appeared at Tess's shoulder. "Mrs. Bravo, your husband wants you. In the office."

It took Tess a moment to realize that "Mrs. Bravo" was herself. "Oh. Certainly." She smiled at the housekeeper. "Thank you, Angie." She turned to Carmen, who was already hard at work on that full plate. "Excuse me."

Carmen waved a plump hand and dug into her thick slice of Rising Sun prime rib.

Zach's office was on the first floor, off the dining room. Tess hurried there, slipping inside to find him at the big cherrywood desk, talking on the phone. He signaled her over, then put the mouthpiece under his chin.

"My folks," he whispered.

Tess herself had no family left to speak of. Her dad had died four years ago, and her mom had passed on just the previous December. But Zach's parents, Elaine and Austin, were still alive and well and living in New York City. They hadn't been able to get away on such short notice.

"It's nice of them to call," she said.

He held out the phone, his palm over the mouthpiece. "Tell them how much you wish they were here."

She took the phone and spoke with Zach's mother and then with his father. Each said how much they regretted not being there and how they wanted to meet her and would try to get out for a visit sometime soon.

"Thank you," Tess replied. "We'd love to see you— anytime." She said goodbye and hung up.

The phone started ringing again the second the handset hit the cradle.

It was one of Zach's two sisters, the one who lived in Philadelphia. She said the same things his parents had said, to Tess first and then to Zach.

When they hung up, he turned to her. "Let's dance."

She put her hand in his and he led her out through the dining room to the great room, where the big rug had been rolled back and the furniture pushed close to the walls. The three-piece band the caterer had brought was playing

"It's Just a Matter of Time." Zach took her in his arms and they moved out on the floor.

A half an hour later, Zach's other sister called. Zach and Tess trooped back into the office to be congratulated some more. The second sister lived in some place called SoHo. Tess made polite noises and listened to the very East Coast sounding voice and wondered how in the world a cattleman like Zach could have come out of such a family.

Edna had told Tess months ago, "Zach's daddy, Austin, only wanted one thing from life—to get out of Wyoming and find someplace *civilized.* Zach was born in New York City. But then Austin made the mistake of letting him come to the ranch for a visit when he was ten. And Zacharius knew the minute he set foot on the Rising Sun that ranching would be his life. He convinced his father and mother to let him come to us three years later and he has pretty much been a fixture at the ranch ever since—except for that stint at Texas A&M after Leila left him. He was an AG major, of course. Even when his grandfather and his parents made him go to college, all he wanted to do was learn about how to raise better beef."

"She says she might come out for a visit real soon," Tess said when Zach hung up the phone from talking to Melinda, the sister from the place called SoHo.

Zach made a snorting noise. "When pigs fly. Melinda considers Wyoming the north end of nowhere. None of our restaurants are interesting enough, shopping opportunities are limited—and she might break a nail. Forget it." He pulled Tess back toward the great room, where he put his arms around her and led her out onto the floor again.

Tess closed her eyes and let herself enjoy dancing with him. She was a little scared about the night to come, but felt sure she would be able to get through it all right. He was a considerate man, after all. They would manage it, and in the morning they would be husband and wife in every way.

It was midnight when the last guest drove off. And another hour had passed before the caterer from Sheridan headed for the highway in her panel truck. Zach had settled up with the woman a while before. Still, out of politeness, Tess stood in the dark yard to watch the woman leave. Then she turned for the house.

Inside, she called quietly for Zach. When he didn't answer, she assumed he was either back in the office for some reason—or already upstairs in their bedroom.

Their bedroom. Her cheeks grew warm at the thought and a thousand fluttery things got loose inside her stomach.

She drew in a deep breath and headed for the stairs.

In the upper hall, she decided to peek in on Jobeth. Pausing outside her daughter's room, she slipped off her shoes and set them on the hall floor. Then, oh-so-quietly, she pushed open the door.

Across the room in the single bed, beneath the window that looked out on the side yard, Jobeth slept. She lay curled in a ball, her lips curved in a contented smile— despite the fact that she'd kicked the covers away and had to be just a little bit chilly. Careful not to disturb her slumber, Tess pulled up the blankets and tucked Jobeth in.

Jobeth snuggled down and muttered something that was almost a word, "Mmnph..." But she didn't open her eyes.

Very lightly, Tess smoothed the feathery bangs from Jobeth's forehead and brushed a kiss there. Then, for a few precious moments more, she stood staring down at her daughter, enjoying that wonderful feeling of lightness that sometimes came over her when she looked at Jobeth. She found herself thinking, Ah, yes. So many mistakes. But this one thing, my daughter. This one thing, I'm doing right...

Finally, when Tess knew she could no longer postpone the short walk down the hall to the master bedroom, she turned and tiptoed out the way she had come. Pausing only to scoop up her shoes from the floor, she went to join her new husband.

He wasn't there.

She felt a moment of sheer relief. His absence meant she could put off what would happen just a little while longer. But then she started wondering where he might be. And then she understood.

He was being thoughtful, giving her a few minutes alone, to prepare herself, before he joined her. With those pesky fluttery things kicking up a ruckus in her stomach again, she began unbuttoning her buttons and slipping out of her beautiful lavender dress.

A few moments later, feeling totally naked though she still wore her slip and all her underwear, she padded to the closet to hang up the dress and collect her waiting nightwear. She was already reaching for a hanger before her mind actually registered what her eyes had seen. Zach's side was bare.

Chapter Four

Moving automatically, Tess hung up her dress. Then, still in her slip, she left the big closet and strode to the double bureau. Slowly, one at a time, she pulled open each drawer on Zach's side.

Every one of them was empty.

Tess stood staring down at all that emptiness and wondered what in the world was going on.

With a small cry of dismay, she shoved a drawer shut. Then, quickly, in succession, she closed the other ones.

It didn't help. She could still see all that emptiness in her mind.

Numbly she turned and walked to the bed. Once there, she clutched one of the posts for a minute, and then she dropped to a sitting position on the quilted maroon counterpane.

Several moments passed, during which she sat hunched over, rubbing her bare arms, confused...and afraid.

Zach did not plan to sleep in the same room with her. Some time after Wednesday night—when he might or might not have seen a thoughtless look she had turned Cash's way—he had decided, without bothering to mention it to her, that he would move to another room.

He must be very angry with her.

But he hadn't seemed angry. He'd been kind and attentive all afternoon and evening. He'd danced with her several times. And they had laughed together often. She remembered clearly how easily he had joked with her, about his family, about his sister from SoHo, who wouldn't come to visit because she might break a nail.

Could he have only pretended to be kind and to joke? Could this be some cruel revenge? Had he seen the look she'd given Cash, correctly read its meaning—and decided to show her exactly what he thought of a woman who could love one man and still agree to wed another?

She shook her head. She couldn't believe that of Zach. He wasn't a vengeful man. If he'd seen by her face that she loved Cash, he'd have confronted her. Or simply called off the marriage.

But whatever he might have done, he wouldn't do something so cruel as this, removing his things from the room they were supposed to have shared—and letting her find out she'd sleep alone when she went to don her wedding negligee.

Yet he *had* done it.

Tess lifted her head and straightened her shoulders.

She had to face him, to find out what he meant by this. He might imagine that she wouldn't dare confront him, because of her shame and guilt at the secrets in her heart.

And to a degree, he would be right. She did feel great shame. And crushing guilt. She didn't *want* to love

Abby's husband. Every day she prayed that the love she felt would fade away. But still, she did love Cash.

And she clung tightly to her belief that no one else knew.

Yet she *had* to confront Zach. If she didn't confront him, they had no marriage. She might as well put everything back in boxes and head for Edna's—not that Edna would take her in, once she learned why it hadn't worked out between her and Zach.

Determined, Tess rose to her feet. She returned to the closet and found her old blue plaid robe in one of the boxes she'd yet to unpack. She pulled it on over her slip and belted it firmly at the waist. Next, she went to the big, battered suitcase that waited by the door to the hall. It contained the rest of the clothes she'd brought from Edna's just today. She found her house slippers and slid them on. Finally she turned to the mirror over the bureau and met her own eyes.

She didn't like what she saw there: worry, misery and guilt. Too much of her life had been wasted, living those emotions over and over again.

For nearly all of the rough years of her marriage to Josh, worry had dogged her. She worried that the landlord would catch her on the stairs and demand the rent today— or else. She worried that Josh would drink away his paycheck before he brought it home. Worried that he would quit his job before he ever got a paycheck. And once he'd quit, she worried that he'd never work again. Josh's dreams had always been so much bigger than anything he ever actually managed to accomplish. And it depressed him, to have to go to work every day at some dead-end job when he wanted to be out drilling the oil well that would make him a millionaire.

He had been a good-hearted man. But still, whenever

Tess thought of him, she remembered the constant, nagging worry she had known during most of her life with him.

She had done what she could to combat the worry. She had worked, whenever she could find something. But with Jobeth so young, it could never be more than part-time. And it was always for minimum wage. And she never had a chance to get anywhere on any job she found, because they inevitably packed up and moved on to someplace that Josh swore would be better.

Wherever they moved, the worry went with them.

The worry had caused the misery, the hopelessness, the growing certainty that they would never get out of the financial hole they had dug for themselves. The only bright spots had been the wonder of having a daughter like Jobeth—and the light of hope that Cash inspired, with his generosity to them.

Three or four years ago, Tess had realized that she didn't love her husband—and she did love Cash.

That had brought the guilt.

Finally, Josh had died. Roughnecking on an oil rig was dangerous work and an accident had killed him. The guilt had gone on, after Josh's death. Because her feelings for Cash hadn't faded.

Still, in the good life she and Jobeth had lived with Edna, much of the worry and all of the misery had slowly melted away.

Until tonight—when she had walked into that half-empty closet and looked in those accusing, vacant bureau drawers. Tonight, the misery and the worry had come crowding back on her, joining her guilt to make the whole world seem bleak and without hope.

She would not live that way. In spite of the mistakes she'd made the first time around, Tess *believed* in marriage. She believed that a man and a woman could and should form a lasting commitment, raise children, help each other through the tough times and share the joys as well.

But she *could* build a life on her own, just herself and Jobeth, if she had to. She was determined that this marriage would be different, *better* than the other. Or she would end it now.

Tess turned away from the face in the mirror and headed for the door.

The minute he saw her, standing in the arch that led to the stairway, wearing a threadbare plaid robe and a look of grim determination, Zach knew he'd handled the situation all wrong.

She said his name, softly, hopelessly. "Zach."

They stared at each other for what seemed like a bleak eternity.

"You moved your things," she said at last, her voice breaking a little. She dragged in a breath and finished, "from the bedroom."

He went to the liquor cabinet, which stood against the wall opposite the windows and the sofa. There, he got out a little false courage, pausing, once he had the bottle in his hand, to hold it up toward her.

"No, thank you," she said.

He shrugged, poured himself a shot and knocked it back. It burned a fortifying trail of liquid heat into his belly. He set the glass down.

She stuck her hands into her pockets and spoke with great effort. "You never said anything about us not sharing a room. When I brought my things on Wednesday, your clothes were there. But now, the closet and the bureau, it's all half empty and I just don't—"

He put up a hand and she fell silent. "Look," he said. "Sit down."

She hovered there in the arch to the central hall, biting her lip, looking at him through wounded eyes.

He felt like some kind of heartless wife abuser. "Please, Tess. Come here and sit down."

She hesitated a moment more and then, at last, she padded across the giant rag rug his grandmother had braided herself forty years before. She went to the sofa, where she perched on the edge like some terrified little bird ready to take flight at the slightest hint of a threat.

She folded her hands on her knees and then she looked at him good and long. "You changed your clothes," she said at last. "That's where you were, when I came in from outside a while ago."

"Right." He gave a quick glance down at his Wranglers and flannel shirt, shrugging as he had when she refused the drink he'd offered. "The party's over. I wanted to get comfortable. So what?"

"You know what. You came back down here after I went up. Since everyone left, you've been purposely avoiding me, purposely going wherever I'm not."

He closed his eyes, ran a hand down his face. "I didn't avoid you, Tess. Not really. I didn't think on it much. I was restless, that's all."

"You didn't think on it much?" She looked even more wounded, if that was possible, than before.

"Tess. Listen."

"I am. I'm listening. You tell me. Whatever it is, you just tell me. Okay?"

"Okay."

"Good."

"Okay."

She waited.

He made himself try to explain. "I, well, I've been alone for a number of years now. As a man, I mean. A single man."

She pressed her lips together, nodded, gave a little cough. "Okay."

He stumbled on. "I, well, I can see I should have thought about you, about how you would take it, when you saw I moved my things. But I didn't. And I do apologize."

She looked down, smoothed her robe over her knees. Then she looked at him again, in rising hope that made her eyes look misty and her skin all sweetly pink. "You apologize?"

"I do. And I hope you'll forgive a man for not knowing how to behave."

She looked away, uncertain, embarrassed.

Damn. She was pretty. A pretty woman. He liked the soft way she could smile and the exotic way her brown eyes tilted up at the corners. He recalled, for some crazy reason, the day that Cash married Abby. Tess had been there, newly widowed, hiding behind the punch bowl, waiting on the guests, trying, it had seemed to him, to make herself invisible.

Abby hadn't allowed that. She'd grabbed him and grabbed Tess and ordered them to dance with each other. He'd done it willingly, smiling at the way the widow DeMarley blushed and got all flustered, thinking that she looked like the type of woman who would make a man the perfect wife—*if* a man was willing to take another chance on marriage.

Which he hadn't been. Not right then, anyway.

But then, in the months that followed, he'd seen her in action. Tasted the food she cooked. Watched the way, whenever she came to the ranch with Edna for a visit, everything suddenly ran smoothly. Mouthwatering meals appeared right on time. There was cleanliness where there had been a layer of grime, order in place of chaos.

She was frowning again. He realized she wanted a little extra reassurance.

"Tess. I am sorry. Please won't you accept my apology?"

Her brow smoothed out. She lifted a hand and put her fingers to her lips, the way she had done the night he'd kissed her. But this time it wasn't because of a kiss. It was a way to gather courage. To ask a question whose answer she probably didn't really want to hear.

She got the question out on a shaky breath. "Why? Why did you change your mind, about...the room? The bed..." She winced and then swallowed. "You know what I mean."

He considered his answer, pondered going straight for the throat, hitting her with something like, I saw that look you gave Cash the other night. And I believe I'll take a pass on making love with a woman who just might be pretending that I'm someone else.

But he couldn't bring himself to do that. She was a good woman, a fine mother—and she had been a loyal wife to that damn dreaming fool, Josh DeMarley. Looking into her sweet, scared face, Zach understood exactly how her love for Cash must shame her. It went against all she held true and right. He didn't doubt that her only consolation in the matter was the belief that no one else knew her guilty secret.

He just couldn't tell her that *he* did know. He couldn't do that to her.

Or to himself.

He was a man, after all. And a man had a right to a

little damn pride. He didn't need to hear how his new bride loved his cousin. Not now. Probably not ever.

Time. That was what they needed. Time to work side by side. Time to forge a real bond. Time to let what she felt for Cash fade by itself.

What makes you think it's going to fade? a cynical voice in his mind demanded.

"Zach?"

He realized he'd made her wait way too long for his answer.

"Zach, please." She stood and dared to approach him, her slippers making no sound as she tiptoed across his grandmother's rug. "You have to tell me why." She stopped three feet from him, close enough that he imagined he could smell that light, flowery perfume she wore, close enough that the soft luster of her skin taunted him, close enough that he couldn't help thinking, Why the hell not just take her to bed? She *is* my wife. As of today, the state of Wyoming says we are joined....

Grimly he kept to his original intention. "I think we need time, Tess."

She stared at him. Then she asked doubtfully, "Is that all? Just...time?"

He nodded. "I got to thinking how we really don't know each other all that well. That we could take our time about this. There's no law that says we have to jump into bed together." As he spoke, he watched her face. She wanted to believe him. Desperately. If time was the only issue, that would mean her secret was safe.

And then she frowned again.

"What?" he demanded.

Haltingly she argued, "But Zach, we *are* married. And it really does seem like married people ought to, um, be intimate. That they should—"

To cut off that dangerous line of reasoning, he invaded her space a little, stepping forward, eliminating what was left of the distance between them. "They should what?"

She stared up at him, her eyes widening. "I..."

"What?"

"I just..."

He'd accomplished his goal: to make her lose her train of thought—but at a certain cost to his own self-control. This close, the scent of her was all around him. He breathed it in, looking at her mouth, thinking of what he *wasn't* going to do. Very slowly, because he wanted to and he had the right and he wasn't going to do anything more, he lifted a lock of her hair and rubbed it between his thumb and forefinger.

She struggled to continue her debate. "I, um, told you I wanted children. I thought...you agreed about that."

"I have a child." The strands of hair felt like silk. Warm silk. "And so do you."

Her breasts rose as she sucked in a big breath. "Well, I know. But I mean, um..."

He knew exactly what she meant. "Children we made together?"

"Yes."

He let go of the silky strands and made himself step back. "If it works out that way, sure."

"Well, but..."

"What?"

"Well, Zach, as I just said, I *do* want more children. I know I told you that more than once. But maybe you didn't really understand. I've always wanted at least three or four."

He had understood. Perfectly. Again, he suggested, "Give it time."

She stared at him. "Time," she repeated. Her eyes

seemed to ask How much time? But she didn't get the question out, which was fine with him. He had no answer to it, anyway.

He decided he could use one more drink. He turned back to the liquor cabinet.

Tess watched him pour the second drink.

She was trying to tell herself that maybe what he suggested wasn't such a terrible idea. They could play it by ear, day to day. She could earn his trust. And a place at his side. And the children she longed for, as well.

And maybe, with time, it wouldn't feel quite so...awkward to imagine the two of them together, in the bed upstairs. Maybe he had grasped the situation better than she had. Maybe he was right. And in the meantime, as they grew to know each other better, she would work hard as mistress of the Rising Sun. She would take care of him and the hands, just as she'd promised. She would have her garden and paint the house. She would be his wife in every way but one.

It wasn't so terrible. She could handle it, she was sure.

And clearly, this had nothing to do with Cash. Nothing at all. Her fears on that score had been groundless.

Zach knocked back the second shot and set down the glass. "Well?"

What else was there to say? Except, "All right, Zach. We'll give it time."

Chapter Five

The next morning, Tess was up well before anyone else. She set right to work whipping up a big breakfast, pausing only to murmur, "Good morning" to Zach when he went out into the predawn chill to tend the animals in the barn and sheds. Angie appeared from the foreman's cottage soon after Zach went out. Tess greeted her and told her to go on back to bed. "I've got things under control, don't you worry."

Angie yawned. "Do I look worried? I'll be out of here tomorrow, in case Mr. Bravo didn't tell you."

Tess paused in her work to smile at the housekeeper. "He did tell me. And we'll miss you."

Angie made a scoffing sound, as a wide grin broke out on her usually serious face. "Right. You cook circles around me, you're neat as a pin and I've never seen a better organizer. I'm not needed here anymore, and we both know it."

Tess tactfully moved the subject along. "Zach did give you a reference, didn't he?"

Angie shrugged. "He did. And a nice one, too. Not that I'll need it. I'm through taking care of other people's houses. Going to spend the rest of my days with my daughter and her family. And if you meant what you said, I believe I will steal another few winks."

"I meant it. You go on."

Moments later, Jobeth came bouncing down the stairs. "Where's Zach? Did he go out already?"

Tess pointed with a spatula toward the barn. Jobeth bounced on out the door. She and Zach came back inside fifteen minutes later, just as Tess was taking the second sheet of biscuits from the oven.

"Jobeth, go ring that bell for the hands," Tess instructed. "And then get washed up. Quick time."

Jobeth flew out to the front porch. The dinner bell clanged long and loud. A few minutes later, everyone but Angie was seated at the big pine table in the kitchen, passing mounds of biscuits and a huge bowl of gravy, helping themselves to orange juice and breakfast sausage.

Tess looked around the table and felt pretty good. Both Zach and Jobeth were packing it away. And the three hands had droopy eyes, hair still wet from a morning wake-up dunking—and full mouths.

"This is great, Mrs. Bravo," said Beau Tisdale, the youngest of the three. He sandwiched the praise between one huge bite and the next.

Zach had told Tess about Beau and his family. Not that long ago, the Tisdales had run their own ranch in the shadow of the Big Horns. But in the end, low beef prices and high bank loans had done them in. Much of the Tisdale land belonged to the Bravos now. And their youngest son worked for Zach.

It wasn't the first time Tess had heard a story like that. In fact, she had pretty much lived that story herself. When her father died, her own family's ranch had been badly in debt. Her mother had asked Tess and Josh to come home and help her out. Josh had been in the middle of one of his big schemes, one that he swore would come in a gusher. He said they just couldn't afford to go back then—and anyway, he wasn't about to waste another minute of his life knee-deep in cow manure.

Tess's mother hadn't been equipped to run the place herself. Soon enough, she had been forced to sell everything to pay off the debts.

So Tess felt a certain compassion for Beau. She gave him a smile. "I'm pleased you enjoy the food."

He grinned back at her. "I surely do."

"I want to head out to the North Pasture," Zach said flatly. "So eat up."

Beau turned his attention back to his plate. Confused, Tess looked down the table at Zach. "You won't be going to church with me and Jobeth?"

For months now, Zach had shown up at Edna's door every Sunday, smelling of soap and aftershave, wearing his best boots, ready to squire her off to the little white-trimmed brick building over on Antelope Street where the Reverend Applegate presided. Until just now, Tess had assumed that today would be the same. However, after last night, she supposed she'd better not assume anything when it came to her new husband.

"I'll be back by nine and ready to go by nine-thirty." His tone was a little cold and his expression stern.

Still, he *would* go. A smile broke across her face. "Oh, good."

And something happened. His stern look melted. He smiled at her. And she smiled back. For one lovely moment, there was only the two of them, a warm feeling passing back and forth, each to the other.

And then Lolly Franzen, one of the other two hands, who sat to Beau's right, let out a small noise that just might have been a snicker. Tess blinked and looked at the man, who obviously thought he'd just witnessed some romantic interchange between smitten newlyweds.

Zach was looking stern again. "Got a problem, Loll?"

"No, boss. No problem. Nosirree, no way."

"Good. Finish up. Work's waiting."

Lolly dug into the rest of his meal as if his life depended on how fast he could get it down.

The men were gone in ten minutes. Jobeth sulked a little at not being allowed to go with them, but once they'd cleaned up the table, Tess sent her out to hand-feed Bozo and that perked her up. When she came back in, a full hour and a half later, Tess ordered her upstairs to wash and put on one of her two nice dresses.

The phone rang as Tess was bustling around the bedroom, getting herself ready to go. It was Edna.

"Well," the older woman said cheerfully. "And how is Mrs. Bravo this morning?" The simple question had a thousand shades of meaning, most of them concerning the wedding night just past.

Tess had no intention of letting Edna know she'd spent her wedding night alone. She infused her voice with warmth and happiness. "Mrs. Bravo is just fine."

"I am so glad."

"And how are you?"

Edna sighed. "Well. Maybe just a *little* lonely. I'm used to having you to talk to—and Jobeth running in and out."

Tess caught sight of herself in the bureau mirror and smiled at her own reflection. She had figured this would probably happen. "You could come and stay here—for a while, or even indefinitely. You know that."

"Oh, no. Absolutely not. You have a right to your own life and I—"

"Edna. You are a part of my life. A big part. And Zach and Jobeth feel the same way." She thought, suddenly, of exactly what it would mean if Edna came to stay. She would surely find out that the new Mr. and Mrs. Bravo slept in separate beds.

Edna sighed again. "No. I couldn't. I'll be fine. I have my dream, don't I? This beautiful house that Cash bought me." Cash had given Edna the house during her illness, two years ago. "It's just that I'm a little down, getting used to the quiet around here without you and Jobeth. And I just called Abigail. She and Cash are taking off again— and my grandson, too, of course."

Cash made money in a variety of investments, from oil to real estate to computer software. If he heard of a good thing, he put money in it. And Abby, with her degree in finance from CU, was his business manager. They were forever packing up and heading for Reno or Cheyenne, to meet with Cash's wheeler-dealer friends. "Oh, well." More sighing. "I suppose I'll just be going over to church all on my own."

Tess took the hint. "We'll be there to pick you up."

She could actually *hear* Edna's grateful smile. "You're a dear."

"Be ready to go at ten-fifteen."

"You know I will."

At church, before and after the service, both Tess and Zach received endless congratulations and wishes for their long-lasting happiness. Tess smiled and said "Thank you" so many times, it began to seem to her as if the two words were nonsense sounds, without any real meaning at all. More than once, as she was saying those two words, she cast a quick glance at her husband. He was smiling and saying "Thank you," too. He seemed to be taking it all in stride. Really, no one in the world would have imagined anything at all wrong between him and his new bride.

Tess caught her thoughts up short. There *was* nothing wrong. They had agreed to take it slow, that was all. In their situation—not a love match but a practical pairing—taking it slow made perfect sense.

Or so she kept telling herself.

After church, Edna insisted they all come over to her place for lunch. She flitted around them, serving them, clearly excited over their newlywed state.

At last, Zach told her, "Settle down, Edna. All your fussing and fluttering will put me off my feed."

Edna put a hand to her throat. "Oh, I know. I'm terrible. But I can't help it. Seeing you two together. Seeing how *perfect* you are for each other, well, it does my heart good, that's all."

Tess felt a silly blush starting, moving up her neck toward her cheeks. She didn't realize she was staring at Zach until he turned and looked at her.

"We're very happy," he said, and he smiled.

Tess wondered how in the world he could hide his feelings so completely. In her mind's eye, she saw all those people at church, shaking her hand, hugging her, wishing her well. She felt like a complete phony. *Taking it slow* was just an excuse, and she knew it. Her husband didn't want her and her practical marriage was a total sham. She blinked and looked down at her plate.

"Mom?" Jobeth, always sensitive, asked in concern. "Are you crying?"

She wasn't, of course. She never cried. Not in years. She looked up and smiled. "I'm just fine."

Edna turned to Jobeth. "She's a bride, honey. It's a beautiful, magical, *emotional* time."

They got back to the ranch at a little after two. Zach took one of the pickups and drove out to the North Pasture again, this time letting Jobeth accompany him. They returned two hours later.

"We're branding tomorrow," Jobeth explained proudly as she set the table for dinner. "Way out in the North Pasture. Nate and Sonny will be there. Nate will handle the irons and Sonny will help in the crowding pen." Sonny Kane was Meggie's cousin. He and his wife and children lived and worked at the Double-K with Nate and Meggie. "Since this will be my first branding," Jobeth continued, "I'm gonna do the tallying. Zach says we have to be out by four in the morning, so—"

Tess knew a snow job when she heard one. "Jobeth. Stop."

Jobeth glanced up from her task, her eyes wide and innocent. "What?"

"Did Zach tell you that you could help with the branding tomorrow?"

Jobeth took a napkin, folded it with great care into a triangle and tucked it beside a plate. "Zach said that for a person's first time, she usually does the tallying."

"That was not my question, and you know it."

Jobeth looked down, up, sideways—anywhere but at her mother.

Tess said gently, "Tomorrow is a school day."

Jobeth groaned. "Mom!" She stretched out the word so it sounded as if it had several syllables in it. "We are ranchers now. Sometimes, when you're a rancher, you have to miss a little school."

Tess hid her smile. Jobeth had a point. As she grew older and acquired the thousand and one skills a true rancher needed, she would make herself invaluable. And she would be allowed to miss some school—all this assuming that Tess and Zach stayed married, of course, and that Jobeth got her chance to grow up here.

Jobeth was frowning. "Mom? What's the matter?"

"What? Nothing."

"We were talking. I was explaining to you how I have to miss school tomorrow and you just…stopped listening."

Tess pushed the nagging worry about her relationship with Zach out of her mind. "I apologize for woolgathering."

Jobeth pulled a face. *"Woolgathering?"*

"That's another word for not listening, for letting your mind wander."

"Oh."

"But whether I was woolgathering or not, you are not missing school. Not this time."

Jobeth moaned—and then fastened on the part of her mother's statement that she liked. "But later. When I know more. When Zach and the other guys can't get along without me. I just might have to miss some school then, right?"

Tess ran a finger down the center of her daughter's forehead, tracing the natural line where her bangs tended to part. "Yes. I imagine so."

Jobeth heaved a sigh. "It's better than nothing, I guess."

Zach went out again after dinner, and didn't return until after nine. Tess, in the great room with her gardening book open on her lap, heard the pickup drive in. He must have hung around the barn and sheds for a while, because it was a half an hour later when she heard him come through the back door.

Tess closed her book, marking her place with the scrap of paper on which she'd been scribbling possible garden layouts. From the sofa where she sat, she could see the central hall and the foot of the stairs. She waited, watching.

Sure enough, Zach appeared in his stocking feet, headed for the stairs.

"Zach?" She stood.

He stopped with one heavy wool sock on the first step, and looked at her through the arch that separated the two rooms. She moved toward him, carrying her book, and stopped inside the hall arch, about five feet from where he waited to see what she wanted.

She tried a smile. "Muddy boots, huh?"

He shrugged. "I left them by the back door."

"Best place for them."

"Yeah. I guess so." He waited, his hand on the banister, ready to get out of there as soon as she told him why she'd stopped him.

The stranger I married, she thought with more self-pity than she should have allowed herself.

But then he actually smiled and gestured at the book she held. "Planning your garden, huh?"

She returned his smile. "I should have done this in January or February. The planning, I mean. Well, I *did* plan in January. But for the garden at Edna's. And that was different. Smaller, for one thing. And then, the windbreak, with the fence and the surrounding houses and all, was so much more effective than I'm going to get here at the ranch...." She realized she was babbling and cut herself short. "Anyway, I'll work it out."

"I know you will." He looked at her for a long moment. It seemed a warm look. But how could she know for sure? Then he shook himself and glanced down at the mud that spattered his jeans and shirt. "I'm a mess. Gotta go." He started to move.

"Wait."

He stopped.

She rushed on, before he could leave her. "Tomorrow will be a branding day. Is that right?"

"You bet."

"In the North Pasture?"

"Right."

"I'm not sure where that is exactly. I wonder...could you draw me a map?"

He frowned. "A map."

"Could I get my Tercel out there, do you think? It's got four-wheel drive."

"Sure, you could. But I don't—"

"Then after I make certain Jobeth catches the bus, I thought I'd load up some food and come join you."

He said nothing for a moment. Then he told her gently, "You don't have to do that. If you'll just pack us up something we can take along, that would be more than—"

"Zach."

"What?"

"I *want* to do it."

He stared at her, looking wary and maybe a little hopeful, too.

For the first time since that brief, shared glance at the breakfast table that morning, she felt warmly toward him. "Zach. You never know. I might even pitch in. I've been in on my share of brandings, in case I didn't mention it."

He seemed bemused. "Well."

"Well, what?"

"All right. We can always use an extra hand."

Since Sonny's wife, Farrah, had come along to do the tally of the calves they branded and to handle the vaccine gun, they let Tess work the crowding pen with Sonny and Lolly. It was the dirtiest, toughest job of the branding process, during which they not only branded the calves, but also vaccinated them and castrated the males. Between them, Tess and the others chased and shoved and wrestled the penned calves into the calf table, a special working chute that could be rotated sideways, laying the calf in position to take the brand.

Tess proved herself proficient at the job—and then, when they switched positions for a while, she got to take Beau Tisdale's place and hold a few hind legs. Hind leg holding could be quite challenging. You had to hold tight, or the one doing the castrating could get cut or kicked. And with all the stress the calves endured under the iron and the knife, they tended to be incontinent. So the hind leg holder got to hold tight—*and* dodge flying streams of manure at the same time.

Still, branding was its own kind of fun, with everybody working hard as a team to get the job done.

They took a beer break at nine. To them, after all, it was the middle of the day. And they stopped for lunch at eleven, with only about fifteen calves to go. Tess realized they were stopping for her sake, since she'd brought the food out there. They could have just finished up and ridden on home to eat.

But whether lunch out in the pasture was necessary or not, it was fun. Everyone said it made scrabbling around in the dust, manhandling cattle almost worth it, for a hot meal like this one.

"Where's Meggie?" Zach asked, between bites. "I can't believe she'd let a branding go by without at least showing up to see that we're doing things right."

"She's home," Nate said, somewhat grimly. "She was up half the night with Jace. I told her she was spending her day catching up on her rest."

Farrah laughed. "You know how she is. She kept insisting I should stay with Jace and Davy." Davy was Farrah's three-year-old. "Meggie swore she'd take it easy, if Nate would just let her come, that she'd handle the tally and the vaccine guns."

Nate added, "I said she'd take it easy, all right. In bed. Period."

Farrah chuckled some more. "Nate practically had to tie her up to get her to change her mind."

"Tell her we missed her," Zach said.

Nate snorted. "As if that'll make her feel better. You know how she is. She's not going to be happy until she's back on that bay mare of hers, running the rest of us ragged."

Zach was grinning. "Well, we've got several more days of this, between your place and the Rising Sun. You think you'll keep her home through all of it?"

"I'll keep her home," Nate said darkly. "If I have to lock her in the bedroom."

Zach kept on grinning. "She'll climb out the window."

Nate was not amused. "Don't say it. Don't even think it."

Tess watched the interplay between the cousins, thinking how handsome Zach really was—in a rugged, no-frills sort of way, with his sun-toughened skin, strong cheekbones and hawklike nose.

But then again, maybe he did have a frill or two. If you looked close. He'd taken off his hat and his thick brown hair shone golden in the sun. And there was a dimple in his chin—a cleft, Tess mentally corrected herself. Men didn't have dimples, they had clefts. And then he had such a nice mouth, as all the Bravos did. Kind of full for a man. A mouth that made a woman think about kissing it.

Strange. All those months they'd been seeing each other, she'd never thought much about Zach's mouth, let alone about *kissing* Zach's mouth. Truth to tell, because of her feelings for Cash, she'd tried *not* to think about kissing Zach. It had just been something she knew would happen someday, if things kept on between them. She supposed she had looked at it as kind of a necessity. He would kiss her. They would make love. And maybe they'd have children—which she saw as the real goal.

But now, the goal was…postponed, to say the least.

And here she was, watching him razz his cousin out in the North Pasture, and thinking about kissing him just for kissing's sake alone.

As if he could feel her watching, Zach started to turn. Tess saw his head move and managed to look out across the pasture before he actually caught her looking. And then she felt foolish, for turning away. She might have simply smiled at him.

And he might have smiled in return.

Tess decided to head back to the house before the others. She had some washing to do, and she wanted to get the dinner under way. And then, once Jobeth got home, they would drive into town to the garden shop, where Tess would buy the equipment she needed, along with a few flats of seedlings to get things going.

The others were already back at the corral when she

got in the car to go, but Zach broke away and came running over. He skimmed off his hat and leaned in her window. "Hey. That was good. Thanks."

She couldn't help teasing, "The food, you mean—or the great hand I've got with a hind leg?"

"Both." He gripped the ledge of her open window and looked down at the Tercel. "How did you manage to get out here in this thing?"

"It was iffy going, now and then. But I made it, as you can see."

His brows drew together. "How long have you had this car?"

She laughed. "Too long."

He stepped back. "Well. The rest of us should be home soon."

"Fine. After Jobeth gets back from school, I'm going to town to the garden shop. So if you get in later than you expect, and I'm not there—"

"I understand. You'll need money."

She hadn't even thought of that. She had a little money of her own and had expected to spend some of it. "No, really, I—"

"In my room. There's a money clip. Top dresser drawer, in back. You'll find several hundred in cash there, for emergencies. Hell. I didn't even think about this. You have any credit cards?"

She shook her head, the old shame rising. She'd been Josh DeMarley's wife, after all. They'd lived hand-to-mouth, paycheck to paycheck. Once, during the first years of their marriage, they'd had a few credit cards. Josh had run them past their limits and then, about five years ago, he'd ended up declaring bankruptcy. After that, no credit card company in the world would have been crazy enough to extend credit to them.

Zach went on, "I'll see about getting you a card on my Visa account, at least. And in the next week or two, we'll have to go in to the bank and put you on my checking account."

"I have a checking account."

He smiled. "Don't get prickly. We never discussed this money thing, and we should have. You need to get on my account. So you have access to my money, when you need it."

"I do not need access to your money."

"Tess." He said her name gently, carefully. "You're my wife."

She almost said it: No, I'm not. Not really. Not completely your wife. But somehow she held it back. She slid her hands up to twelve and then back out to ten and two on the steering wheel. "I want to get going. And you're needed at the corral."

He glanced over his shoulder. "Right." He backed away from the door. "Well, see you at the house, then."

"Yes. All right."

He stuck his hat back on his head and then stood there, watching, as she shifted into gear and drove off.

Once he was behind her, she caught sight of him in her rearview mirror. He was still standing there, staring after her. Finally he seemed to shake himself. He turned to join the others.

Tess focused front again, and came up to the gate. She stopped to open it, her mind stuck, for some silly reason, on the image of him standing there, staring after her.

He had seemed a little lost, a little unsure.

As if he didn't quite know how to deal with her.

And he probably didn't, she thought, as she got back in the car, drove through the gate, and then stopped again to close it behind her. Really, for all their caution with each other, they had kind of jumped into the marriage when it finally came down to it. Between the proposal and the wedding there had been exactly six days. They'd never even taken the time to talk about things like money. Or sex.

Or secrets.

She slid behind the wheel again and shifted into gear. The car started down the rutted dirt road.

Secrets. Well, Zach was never going to know her secrets. And that would make it all the harder for them to become close.

Theirs was simply not your average marriage—which had to be just as confusing for him as it was for her.

Too often, he did seem like a stranger. Still, for all the distance he kept between them, he was a good man who treated her with courtesy and kindness. With the exception of his body, he seemed willing to share all he had with her.

And yet, in spite of his courtesy and kindness, she had felt bitterness toward him. She'd felt it more than once in the brief time since their wedding night. Bitterness was a danger. Bitterness could kill any chance of closeness before it could even be born. She knew *that* from hard experience.

Tess bumped over a particularly bad rut. The car bottomed out, the pan scratching along the ridge of the rut, the transmission letting out an ugly groaning sound as she shifted down from second to first. She willed the old car to keep going, to please just get her home.

And she vowed, no more bitterness. No more bad attitudes. No more self-pity. She would be Zach's wife on his terms, and have some faith that they'd truly find their way to each other in the end.

Chapter Six

Three days later, in the afternoon, Zach took Tess into town. They visited the bank and his insurance agent. Before they went home, Tess and Zach had a joint checking account, Tess had signed on for a Visa card and she and Jobeth had full health coverage.

Then, when Saturday rolled around, Tess found herself in the cab of the blue Chevy pickup on the way to Sheridan with her daughter and her husband. When they came back that evening, Zach and Jobeth were still in the pickup—but Tess was driving a brand-new Suburban, a roomy 4X4 station wagon on a pickup chassis.

"Oh, Zach, it's too much," Tess had protested when she saw the Suburban for the first time, so big and shiny and new on display in the car lot. "You can't—"

He cut her off in his firmest voice. "I can. And you need it. That Tercel was a great little car—at one time.

But for your purposes now it's too old, too small and way too close to the ground.''

When it came time to deal with all the paperwork, Zach wrote an enormous check, paying half in cash—to cut down on the interest, he said. After that, he signed loan forms for the balance. Then he handed the pen to Tess.

She stared at him, not understanding.

He pointed at the next form. ''So the registration will be in your name.''

She thought again of how much the car cost. ''Oh, that's not necessary. Truly, I—''

Zach took her hand and wrapped it around the pen. ''Sign. Right there on that line.''

His touch, so warm and rough and sure, shocked her to her toes. Since he touched her so seldom, each slightest physical contact had started to take on great importance.

''Sign, Tess.''

Rather numbly, she did.

After that, they went out to dinner. Then Tess drove her new Suburban back to the Rising Sun, loving the steady purr of the engine, smelling that incredible new-car smell, and swearing to herself that she would work her fingers to the bone to do what she could in return for all that Zach had given her.

That night, after she put Jobeth to bed, Tess sat in the great room sewing patches onto the knees of a pair of Jobeth's jeans. Soon enough, she heard Zach come in through the back door from his final rounds of the barn and sheds. She knew his routine, and went on with her mending, hardly listening for the sound of his footfalls. He might pause in the kitchen, to drink a glass of water at the sink. But after that, he would go straight for the stairs and head up to his room. He always did.

Or at least, in the week since their wedding, he always had.

But this time, he didn't turn for the stairs. Tess almost poked her finger with her needle when she realized he was headed her way. He stopped just outside the room where she sat. She kept her head bent over the mending, but still, she could feel him there, in the arch to the hall.

"Always busy."

She realized she'd been holding her breath and let it out slowly, so he wouldn't know. Then she looked up and met his eyes. They shared a smile. She held up her mending. "Jobeth. She swears she doesn't walk around on her knees, but you couldn't prove it by me."

He laughed, a warm, friendly sound. Her heart felt featherlight.

"Listen, I..." His sentence died without ever really getting started.

She wanted to urge him to fully enter the room, to sit down, to *talk* to her. But she didn't want to push, either. If he wanted to come in, he would.

He moved forward. One step. And then another, until he stood over her. "I wanted to talk to you a little about Jobeth."

She nodded, very casually, and kind of tipped her head toward the sofa, in an invitation that he could accept or reject without saying a word. He did neither. That is, he didn't sit. But he didn't leave, either.

He strode to the woodstove over by the interior wall, knelt, opened the side door and stirred the coals with the poker. Then he added a couple of logs from the wood box nearby. She watched him, admiring the strong breadth of his back and the way it tapered down to his narrow, hard waist.

When he had finished with the fire, he rose and turned to face her.

"What about Jobeth?" she asked, wondering all of a sudden if he had some kind of problem with her daughter's behavior.

He must have read her expression. "Relax. It's nothing wrong."

"Good. Then what?"

"Well…" He frowned, as if choosing his words with great care. "The truth is, she's been after me."

Tess stuck the needle in the cloth and set her mending in her lap. "After you? For what? To let her quit school and take up cowpunching full-time?"

He grinned. "Not quite."

"But almost."

"No, truly. It's something else."

"What?"

He put his hands into his back pockets, then immediately took them out and folded his arms over his chest.

"*What?*"

He finally got it out. "She wants her own horse."

Tess sat back in her chair, thinking that she should have known.

Zach raised a bronze eyebrow. "What do you think?"

Tess was thinking of the Suburban and what he had spent on it. And now this. He wanted to give her daughter a horse.

"Tess?"

She hedged, "Don't you think Jobeth's a little young?"

Zach came down firmly in Jobeth's behalf. "She's eight. Abby had her own horse at eight—or maybe even at seven, now I think about it."

"But Abby was born here at the ranch. Jobeth hasn't been riding that long."

"Tess, she's a fast learner. You know she is."

Tess had seen her daughter ride. And Zach was right. Jobeth was a natural horsewoman. Still, Tess felt that she and her daughter had taken way too much from him already. She felt a little guilty to consider taking even more. She wanted to draw the line somewhere—for a while, at least. Until she and Zach knew better where they stood with each other.

"Zach, you just can't keep *giving* us things."

"Sure, I can."

"But we can't possibly pay you back."

He frowned a little. "Wait a minute. You're my wife. Jobeth is my stepdaughter. What I have is yours."

She stared at him. The basic problem between them seemed to hang in the air, unsaid—the little problem of the separate beds they slept in, of the way they were always so formal with each other, of the way he avoided her most of the time. Of whether their marriage was really a marriage at all.

She considered the wisdom of going for broke. Of laying it all out there. Of saying again that she didn't feel they were truly married, since they were so careful and polite with each other, since they didn't even share a bed.

Of course, if she went for broke, she'd be taking the chance they'd end up talking about Cash.

She cringed at the thought of that.

No. They'd only been married a week, today. She'd agreed to give it time. And she would. Whether that amounted to cowardice or wisdom, she had no idea.

Zach spoke again. "You work damn hard, Tess. Harder, even, than I expected you would. You're never idle. You're either cleaning or cooking or working in your garden. And at night, you sit in here, mending and planning what other projects to tackle, working some more."

His words pleased her, reinforced her decision to remain silent for now on the deeper issues. She admitted, smiling, "I like to work."

"And people get paid to work. Do you want a salary?"

"No. Of course not, I'm—"

He finished for her. "—my wife. And my wife gets the benefit of what I have. She gets decent insurance and a decent vehicle—to help her do her work more efficiently. Just like my stepdaughter gets a horse, when she's ready for one. I'm not a fool, Tess. I see the potential Jobeth has. She takes to life on the Rising Sun like a duck to a pond. She's a responsible girl. And she's ready for the responsibility of training her own horse."

Tess stared at him, so touched by what he'd just said that she couldn't come up with more arguments.

"Come on, Tess," Zach said when the silence stretched out too long.

She let out a breath, puffing her cheeks as she did it. "I suppose you've already picked out the horse?"

"Yeah. A nice chestnut gelding. Four years old, part Arabian. Green broke, but that's about all. Jobeth really would have to train him. I'd help her some, of course. And Tim said he'd keep an eye on her progress, as well." Tim Cally was the Rising Sun's third hand. He'd been a Bravo employee for over three decades. An old man now, he could still spend a day in the saddle when the ranch needed him. But he took it a little easier than Beau and Lolly as a general rule, helping out around the barn and sheds, mending tack, repairing machinery and handling any animal doctoring that didn't require a real vet.

Tess still just wasn't sure. "How about if we wait another year? Until then, she can still ride that sweet, old mare you picked out for her."

Zach smoothed his hair back with his hand—and kept

to the goal. "Tess. I believe she is ready. And the gelding's a good animal. Smart and quick, but no meanness. Horse-ornery, now and then. But you want them to have a little damn spirit."

Tess opened her mouth to voice more objections. But he looked so hopeful—hopeful for the sake of Jobeth.

His eyes coaxed. His words cajoled. "Come on, Tess. Give the kid a break."

Tess made a noise in her throat and picked up her mending again. She knew exactly what was going on here. If she said no now, then Jobeth would come after her next. And probably Tim, as well. She wouldn't have a moment's peace until she gave in.

And she did trust Zach's judgment when it came to Jobeth. He was watchful and protective of the child. He wouldn't let her come to harm.

He'd just...done so much already, for the two of them. In spite of his generous words about how hard she worked, Tess felt it would be impossible for her contribution to the marriage to ever equal his. And what if it just didn't work out between them in the end? Then Jobeth would have to give up the horse. How much worse would it be to give it up than never to have had it in the first place?

"That garden of yours is looking good," Zach said, pulling out all the stops.

She looked up at him, saw his coaxing smile—and couldn't resist playing along with his game to butter her up. "Tim put up the wire fence for me. And it took me forever to turn and till that ground. Lots of clay in it. Maybe I could open a little pottery shop in my spare time. Throw a few bowls and such."

He chuckled right on cue.

She bent her head and took a stitch, and then another,

drawing the needle through the cloth with precision and care. Then she shot him a look from under her lashes. "I've put in corn as a windbreak. That should help some, and a hedgerow, too. And you know the beds had to be raised good and high. That was more work. But there's no other choice, with the gully-washers we get sometimes."

"You're right," he said. "No other choice."

"But it's coming along."

"I can't wait to taste the results."

She looked up, a more direct look than before. "I know what you're doing."

If he'd had his hat in his hand, he would have been twisting the brim. "She's ready, Tess."

At that moment, Tess felt almost tenderly toward him. She wished they were intimate, just to have the right to touch him. To rise from her chair and put her hand on his arm.

When she spoke, her voice came out a little husky. "You're good to her. So good. Her own father..." She looked down, took a stitch, wondered if she'd said too much.

"What?"

She met his eyes again.

He commanded, softly, "Say it."

She chose her words with great care. "They didn't...understand each other. He wanted to lasso the moon for her. But Jobeth, well, you just can't *dazzle* Jobeth. She didn't want the moon. More than once, he brought her home fancy dolls, dolls with beautiful painted faces, all dressed up in gorgeous clothes, dolls that cost a lot more than we could afford. She would say thank-you and she would really try to mean it. But all she wanted was for him to get us an apartment that allowed pets. So she could have a kitten, you know?''

He nodded. Then he asked, even more softly than before, ''And what about you?''

She looked down at her mending, and then up at him. ''Me?''

''Can you be...dazzled?''

She stared at him, her pulse all at once rocketing into high gear. What did he mean by *dazzled?* Did he mean something about Cash? If any man could be called a dazzler of women, that man would be Cash Bravo.

But then she breathed easier. Her heartbeat slowed. Zach had gone to school in Medicine Creek, after all. And so had Josh. Of course, Zach had to mean Josh.

Tess was aware of a deep sadness then. She thought of Josh that first time she'd seen him, the day he came to work at her father's ranch. She'd never seen a man so handsome, with those green eyes of his and that devilish smile. He'd had an aura about him. Something that seemed to make the air shimmer around him. An aura of risk. Of wildness. Of things of which her parents were not going to approve. She'd been just seventeen. And he had been almost thirty.

Zach prodded, ''Well?''

She kept her head high and answered honestly. ''Yes. I have been dazzled. Foolishly. Dazzled. But Jobeth isn't so easily fooled. All she wanted was a cat. And now she's got a whole barn full of cats. There's a furry critter everywhere she turns. And you...''

''I what?''

''You never come up on her fast. You take your time. You let her come to you. And you never tried to give her a doll. Oh, no. If you give her something, it's exactly what she wants.''

He was silent. Then he said with a slight smile, "Like a horse."

She made a little humphing sound. "So. We're back to the point."

"Is that a yes?"

She tried to look her most severe. "Do I have a prayer of saying no and making it stick?"

"Well now, you're her mother and you're the one who—"

"Just answer the question, Zach."

He looked abashed. "No, ma'am. Probably not."

She knew she was beaten. Still, she said, "Give me a little time. To think it over."

"Well, sure." He frowned. "How much time would that be?"

"A few days?"

"All right, then. Three days."

For the next three days, Tess could feel the weight of her daughter's yearning. Nothing was said. Jobeth knew better. She had let Zach fight this battle for her, and she wouldn't step in herself unless it appeared that the prize was truly lost.

But Jobeth couldn't keep the hope from her eyes. Over and over, Tess would look up from the sink or the stove to find her daughter's gray-blue gaze on her.

Say yes, say yes, those eyes seemed to chant. Tess would smile and go on as if she noticed nothing. In the end, she knew she couldn't deny such desire. And in her heart, Tess did agreed with Zach: Jobeth was ready for her own horse.

Still, Tess wanted the time to change her mind. And she felt it only fitting that her daughter should wait and

wonder a while. A big dream like this shouldn't come
true too easily.

On the third night, the night when Tess was to give him
the answer on the matter of Jobeth's first horse, Zach
brought an armload of wood with him when he came in
for the last time. He went straight through the kitchen and
central hall to the great room, where he knew Tess would
be sitting. He strode right to the wood box and dropped
in the logs. Then he picked up the poker, opened the stove
door and prodded the coals a bit. After that, he shoved in
a log and shut the stove door.

He stood, turning to face Tess. Their eyes met.

He thought she looked really good, sitting there so quietly with her knitting. The light from the lamp at her side
gave her hair a curried shine. She had an inner peace to
her, a calmness inside herself that he'd always admired.
So different than a lot of women.

Sometimes, lately, looking at Tess, Zach would find
himself thinking of Leila, his first wife. Remembering.
Comparing a little, maybe. Leila was a woman who never
could sit still. You wouldn't have found her sitting in the
great room knitting happily away in total silence, not in
a thousand years.

He had loved Leila. The kind of love he'd thought
would never die. It had seemed to him that she had cut
his heart out and taken it with her when she left.

But that had been so long ago. And now, looking at
Tess, he could hear his heart. Beating a little too fast right
inside his own chest. Leila didn't have it, after all.

And the point was not to go losing it again.

Tess looked over those flying knitting needles and
smiled. Zach gestured toward the blue wad of yarn that

was gradually taking the shape of a tiny foot. "What's that?"

"Booties. For Jace. I'm going to make a little hat, as well. And a sweater. I made the same set for Tyler Ross and Meggie admired it, so I thought I'd make one for her baby, too." She set the knitting aside and folded her hands in her lap.

Zach was pretty sure he'd get the answer he wanted tonight, but he felt a little nervous anyway. If Tess did say no, he would have to back her up. He would have to face the disappointment in Jobeth's eyes. He didn't look forward to that. Probably he had too damn much pride when it came to Jobeth. Pride that he had never let her down. Pride that she had taken to him so completely, that she ran to do the tasks he set her, that she looked up to him as if he had all the answers to all the questions ever asked.

Once he had let himself imagine that Starr would be like Jobeth. But instead, she was down in San Diego, cutting school all the time, hanging out with troublemakers and generally driving her mother crazy.

Tess coughed politely into her hand.

Zach realized he was stalling and bestirred himself. "It's been three days. Since we talked about that horse."

"Yes. It has."

"Have you come to a decision?"

"I have." She looked so serious. For a moment, he feared the wrong answer was coming. But then he saw the smile that kept trying to pull on the corners of her mouth. "All right," she said at last. "Jobeth can have the horse."

It took him a moment to register her words—and his own relief.

She filled that moment with instructions. "She's to take

it slow. And have supervision. Either you or Tim should be there when she starts to put him through his paces, because she'll need training herself.''

"I promise," he said. "I'll be there."

She looked all soft. Her eyes had a happy shine to them. "I know you will. Thank you."

He felt about ten feet tall. At that moment, the whole world belonged to him and him alone. It was almost as good as when he'd taken her to get the Suburban.

His body stirred as he imagined himself moving forward, closing the distance between them, putting out his hand. She would lay hers in it. He would pull her up, out of the chair and into his arms, her soft, slim body molding all along his. He would lower his mouth to hers.

And when she returned his kiss, he would not know for sure whose face she saw when she closed her eyes…

He looked down at his boots. And then over at the big windows above the sofa. Night had fallen not too long ago; the windows showed only a dark reflection of the room. "You're welcome," he said, and turned for the stairs.

"Zach." Her voice stopped him just before he cleared the arch to the hall.

"Yeah?"

"Good night."

"Good night, Tess." He went on up the stairs to his solitary room.

Jobeth got her horse the next day after school. When Zach took her out to the pasture to catch him, her eyes were shining so bright, it almost hurt to look at her.

For the next three days, as far as Jobeth was concerned, nothing existed but that horse. She named him Callabash, just because she liked the sound of it. She got up in the morning before her mother or her stepfather to give him oats and carrots and she groomed him until Tim Cally swore she was going to wear the hide right off of him.

Bozo, newly branded and now formally a steer, stood in the small pasture on the other side of the barn, mooing forlornly in longing for the attention Jobeth no longer had time to lavish on him.

In the afternoon, with either Tim or Zach looking on, Jobeth worked with Callabash, leading him around the corral on a tether, later tacking him up slowly and carefully, requiring a little help to get the saddle on and all the straps cinched up good—and finally mounting him and riding him in a circle, getting him used to the feel of her on his back.

On Friday, Tess stood at the sink peeling potatoes and stealing glances out the window, where Jobeth rode Callabash at a smart trot around the corral. Both Zach and Tim hung on the fence, watching and calling out occasional instructions.

Grinning in satisfaction at the sight, Tess looked down at her work once more. When she looked up, a sheriff's office 4X4 came rolling into sight from around front. Zach jumped down from the fence. He waved at Jobeth, calling out something that caused the child to smile and wave back. Then Zach got into the 4X4 on the passenger side and the vehicle drove away.

Frowning, Tess wiped her hands on her apron and went out the back door. She crossed the yard to the corral where Callabash still trotted in a circle with Jobeth on his back.

Tim obligingly dropped off the fence when he saw the boss's wife coming toward him.

"What happened?" Tess asked the old man. "I saw the sheriff's car. Is something wrong?"

Tim swiped his hat off and shuffled his feet. "Well,

ma'am. I reckon Zach saw somethin' that shouldn't have been there. Out near the Crazyman Draw, it was. He didn't like it, so he got someone from the sheriff's office out here to have a look, that's all.''

"I don't understand. What did he see?''

"Tire tracks, ma'am. Looked like a pickup and a stock trailer. And dog tracks, too.''

Tess didn't like the sound of that at all. "More rustling, is that it?''

Back at the end of February, eight bred heifers had been stolen from a pasture not far from the ranch buildings. The heifers would have started calving two weeks after the theft, so in effect, that was sixteen head of cattle gone, amounting to several thousand dollars on the hoof. The story had made the front page of the *Medicine Creek Clarion*. Folks in town had speculated about it for weeks afterward. But then the sheriff had found no leads on the culprits. The talk had died down. Zach hadn't mentioned anything about the theft in a while.

Tim said, "Well, we don't know that it's rustlers, ma'am. Zach just wants that detective to have a look.''

Tess thanked the old man just as Jobeth called, "Mom, Mom, look!'' She reined in the gelding. He stopped smooth and easy.

Tess waved. "Real good, honey. He's coming along just fine.'' She thanked the old man and went back inside.

Tess watched for Zach's return. He was gone about two hours. She managed to catch him alone for a moment just before dinnertime. "I saw you leave in the sheriff's car. Tim said there was some problem out by the Crazyman Draw.''

Zach shook his head. "It's just tire tracks. And a bad feeling. Don't worry about it. The detective says he'll write a report—and dig up the pictures of the tracks from the incident in February for comparison.''

''Did the tracks look the same?''

''I thought so.''

''Oh, Zach…''

''It's probably nothing.'' The words didn't match the disquiet in his eyes.

The next day was Saturday. At breakfast, Zach said he thought both Jobeth and her new horse were ready for a little ride around the horse pasture. It was near noon when the big event occurred, so Tess came out to watch, thinking she'd call them in for lunch once Jobeth and Callabash had trotted around a while.

Jobeth rode out smiling, her head high. Callabash looked pretty proud of himself, prancing a little, but not too much. And Jobeth seemed to have him under control.

But then, about halfway to the far fence, something spooked the gelding. He rose up, letting out a neigh of fright and pawed the air. Tess's heart seemed to freeze in her chest. But Jobeth kept her seat as the horse's hooves hit the ground.

Tess almost allowed herself to breathe. Then the horse reared once more, tossing his head. Jobeth slid backward, twisting as she fell. The horse raced away, leaving the child in a small heap on the hard ground.

Chapter Seven

Zach was already halfway there when Tess jumped the fence and started running, too. Tim followed close behind. Tess could hear the old man's heavy footfalls, though all her mind and heart were focused on the little lump that lay so still and defenseless on the ground.

And then the little lump moved. Tess heard a groan. Jobeth sat up. She blinked and looked around.

Zach reached her. He knelt beside her.

When Tess got to them, Jobeth was cradling her left arm, her dirt-streaked face way too pale. Her eyes locked with her mother's—and she immediately began defending her horse. "It's not Callabash's fault, Mom. There was a snake. I swear, there was a snake." She turned her wide, anxious eyes on Zach, who was already searching the rough pasture ground.

Zach rose, took a few steps, then knelt again. "Here it is." He held up a brown-spotted snake with six neat little rattle buttons at the end of its tail. The head had been crushed, no doubt by Callabash's heavy hooves.

A prairie rattler, Tess though. Not as deadly as a diamondback, or as the sidewinders that basked in the Arizona and New Mexico deserts—but deadly enough to make a child very sick at the least. Tess dropped to her haunches beside her daughter. "Honey, did it bite you?"

Jobeth gazed back at her mother in stark fear—but not for herself. "It didn't get me, I swear. But we've got to check Callabash, see if he—"

Tim Cally spoke from behind Tess. "I'll see to the horse." He started off across the pasture to the far corner, where the gelding had backed himself up near the fence and now regarded them all with a look of edgy disdain.

Zach dropped the snake and knelt beside Tess. Tess glanced over at him, all at once aware of him, of the steady grace of his lean body, of the inner calm that seemed to radiate from him. At that moment, she felt like glass, like something that shouldn't move too fast, or she might shatter into a thousand pointed, ugly shards. Gently she smoothed her daughter's hair. "What's the matter with your arm, honey?"

Jobeth held the arm closer, wincing as she did it. "Nothing. It's nothing." The pain in her eyes gave the lie to her brave words.

Zach stood. "We'll have to take her in. Might as well go right to Buffalo. They've got an X-ray machine at the hospital there."

Jobeth whimpered. "No. It's not broke. It *can't* be broke."

Zach looked down at her, a knowing smile tugging at the corners of his mouth. "You're gonna live, Jo. And you'll be riding again, as soon as that arm heals."

She stared up at him in open yearning, *willing* his words to be true. "You promise me?"

He looked at Tess, deferring to a mother's authority. Tess realized they both feared she'd change her mind about Callabash. Some part of her longed to do just that, to make sure that she'd never again have to live through a moment like the one when Callabash had reared up for the second time and she'd seen her only child go bouncing off toward the ground.

But she *would* live through such moments again, especially with a daughter like Jobeth, who would take a lot of physical risks in the process of making herself into a bona fide cowhand.

"Of course you'll ride again," Tess said.

Jobeth wanted more reassurance than that. "But soon," she cried. "Will I ride again soon?"

Tess felt a flare of irritation. Jobeth needed a doctor. It was no time to negotiate the question of when she would be allowed to get back on a horse. "I'll tell you this. You won't ride *ever* if you don't get that arm taken care of."

Jobeth let go of her injury and grabbed her mother by the shoulder. "Say you won't take Callabash away from me."

Tess met her daughter's eyes, amazed at the fierceness she saw there. Jobeth had always been such an easygoing child, a child who took things as they came. Tess had thought that her daughter's composure was simply Jobeth's nature. But maybe more than nature, it had been resignation. Jobeth had known she'd never have the things she really wanted, so what was there to get all fired up about?

Now, she was fired up but good. "Mom. Please. Just say it. Just promise you me you won't take Callabash away."

Tess realized she'd get nowhere fighting her daughter's new fire. She tried a more soothing tone. "All right. I understand that this accident wasn't your fault, or the fault of your horse. You can ride him again, as soon as your arm is okay—as long as you take care of him, and as long as you can handle him." And as long as Zach and I stay married, she couldn't help thinking. Shoving the ugly thought away, she smiled at Jobeth. "I promise you."

Jobeth let out a long, relieved breath. And then she gave in and allowed herself to consider her injury. Her brows drew together in a grimace of pain. "I guess it kind of does hurt. A lot." But then she thought of Callabash again. She turned, looking for Tim. "Tim!" she yelled, when she spotted him, with the gelding, over by the fence. "Is he—?"

Tim made a high sign. "He's okay! Don't you worry none!"

"Come on," Zach said. "Let's get that arm immobilized."

Zach improvised a splint with a piece of board, some newspaper and some strips of cloth, then Tess made a sling using a dish towel. They piled into the Suburban and started off, Zach driving, Tess cradling Jobeth against her side in the seat behind. Long before they reached the hospital, the shock of the accident had completely worn off and poor Jobeth was in considerable pain. But she tried to be brave, huddling against Tess, doing her best not to cry.

At the hospital, the X ray revealed a closed fracture of Jobeth's left arm, midway between her elbow and her wrist. The doctor set the bone, put on a lightweight plastic cast, gave Tess a prescription for pain medication and said Jobeth could go home.

Even woozy from the anesthetic she'd been given when her arm was set, Jobeth had her eyes on the prize. "When will I be better?" she demanded of the doctor. "I mean, better enough to ride a horse?"

The doctor, a gray-haired woman whom Tess had never met before, looked at Jobeth over the tops of the half-glasses she wore. "Barring complications, the cast should come off in about six weeks. Please stay off all four-legged creatures until that time."

Jobeth threw her head back and let out a frustrated moan. "Six weeks! That's forever...."

The doctor chuckled. "Come back in four. I'll take a look at it, and we'll see, though I'm not promising anything."

Jobeth remained far from pleased. "Four weeks is like a *month*."

"Yes, it is," the doctor agreed. "Four weeks is very much like a month."

"I can't stay off Callabash for a month."

"Jo." Zach, watching from the corner, spoke quietly. Jobeth looked at him. He shook his head. She said no more.

Seney's Rexall was open till five-thirty on Saturdays. They made it just in time to fill Jobeth's prescription. On the way home, Jobeth stretched out in back. Tess took the wheel and Zach sat in the front seat with her.

Halfway there, Zach whispered, "She's asleep."

Tess glanced over her shoulder to see her daughter slumped in the seat, dead to the world. Zach caught her eye as she turned to face the road again.

"She's a helluva kid."

"Yeah. She is."

"Aren't you glad we took care of the insurance?"

She nodded. Having health insurance did ease her mind. During her marriage to Josh, she'd lived in a kind of numb dread of some major illness or injury.

But those days were over now, she told herself firmly.

Outside, the sun still hovered above the mountains, though the shadows had begun to claim the coulees and draws. Here and there in the rolling sea of grass and sage, Tess could pick out the shyly drooping heads of yellow bells and the white, starlike blossoms of sand lilies. Oh, yes. Spring had truly arrived at last.

And Tess felt really good. Jobeth would be fine in a matter of weeks. And Zach had been so wonderful, right there with them through the whole ordeal. Tess had always known he would be a man she could count on. But never had she seen that so clearly as today.

In the great room that night after Jobeth had been tucked into bed, Tess sat reading her favorite book on high-yield gardening techniques. She heard Zach come in and listened to his footsteps moving toward the stairs— and then turning her way. He entered the great room, carrying a load of wood, the way he'd done the night he asked for Tess's answer on the matter of the horse.

Zach tossed the wood into the wood box, put some in the fire and then rose and came to stand over her shoulder.

"Today, it was a real spring day." He spoke in a warm tone that had her smiling blindly down at her open book. "Did you notice?"

She kept her gaze on her book, though if anyone had asked, she couldn't for the life of her have said what she was looking at. "Yes. I noticed. I saw wildflowers in the pastures while we were driving home."

"But tonight..." He let his words trail off.

Tess sent a quick, questioning glance back at him.

And he finished his thought. "Tonight, we're getting another last taste of winter."

As if to punctuate his statement, the wind outside rose up and rattled the windowpanes. Tess spared a moment's concern for her garden, hoping it wouldn't get too cold, and wondering if the precautions she'd taken would be enough to protect the tender plants from the biting force of the wind.

"Hmm," Zach said. "Pixie. Early Girl. Beefsteak. Rushmore. Whoever would have guessed there were so many different names for a tomato?"

She realized he was reading over her shoulder and shut the book, shooting him another quick look as she did it. "How about a beer?" The suggestion came to her lips so naturally, she was glad she had made it—even though the minute the words were out, she felt certain he'd decline.

But a miracle happened. He shrugged. "Sounds good."

She almost blurted out, "Honestly?" in frank surprise, but managed to compose herself in time to keep her mouth shut. She stood. "I'll just get it, then."

Instead of waiting for her, he followed after.

They ended up sitting at the kitchen table, a couple of longnecks in front of them, talking at first about Jobeth and what a little trouper she was, and then later about the mysterious tire tracks Zach had seen on Rising Sun land.

He said, "The sheriff's office left a message on the answering machine while we were gone."

"What did they say?"

"The tire tracks from the Crazyman Draw match the ones from February."

"Oh, no."

"Yeah." He fiddled with the label on his bottle of beer. "I've seen tire tracks before, more than once, in the past few months."

"Did you report them?"

"No. Each time I would tell myself it was nothing." He'd peeled the label loose at the corner. Now he smoothed it back in place over the sweating bottle. "We've got a few mining companies who have legal access. And other local ranchers are always free to come and go across Rising Sun land. I told myself it was something like that. I guess I wanted to believe that what happened in February was an isolated incident. But I've been suspicious for a while now."

"Because cattle have turned up missing?"

He looked up from fiddling with the bottle and met her eyes. "You have to know how it is. With twelve hundred head of cattle, there's no way I can remember them all. But they do get familiar. I close my eyes, I can see them. Individual animals. For example, I remember a big red cow, mostly Hereford, with one white foreleg and a speckled udder. And a certain black-baldy with a bad attitude and a half sliced-off ear. I haven't seen either of them in months now." He let out a weary breath. "And I remember which pasture we put them in. And I know they aren't in those pastures anymore. But that's about all I'll ever know, unless they turn up in another pasture—or we find a carcass somewhere. This is not like those heifers we lost back in February, a clearly identifiable group of animals, in a certain place for a certain reason. Most times, when they disappear, it's like a murder with no corpse. Just a few pitiful little clues. Like where did that black-baldy with the cut-off ear go and what are those pickup and trailer tracks doing out in the Crazyman Draw?"

She asked, "Has the sheriff found out anything at all about those heifers?"

He shook his head. "Come on, Tess. Those heifers have been on somebody's table by now. And the calves are born and branded, part of some other man's herd. It's not like the old days, when a rustler had to try to doctor a brand right out on the open range. Not like when a brand had to pass muster in a local stockyard—a place where the brand inspector knew all the brands. Now, sometimes they butcher them right out in the pasture, and load up that beef in the trunk of a car.''

Tess had heard such stories. Still, the thought appalled her. ''You think that's what's happening on the Rising Sun?''

He waved a hand. ''This is smoother. This is modern-day rustling at its smartest. It's somebody who knows the routines around here. Knows where we'll be and when we'll be there. Somebody with a good pickup and a stock trailer—and a stock dog to get the cattle loaded up with a minimum of effort. They're taking under ten head at a clip. And except for those heifers back in February, which they probably just couldn't resist, they're taking stock out of the biggest pastures, where we're keeping lots of animals. Once they get on the road, they're riding the freeways out of state. And unless we catch them red-handed, we'll never know for sure who the hell they are or how they're getting away with it.''

She repeated his words. '''Somebody who knows the routines around here…'''

Zach nodded. ''More than likely, it's one of our own.''

Tess thought of Beau and Lolly and Tim. Of Angie, who'd seemed so dependable. Could it really be one of them? ''But wouldn't you know, if it was one of the hands? I mean, they'd have to have an opportunity, wouldn't they? They'd have to be gone for a while, to do the job.''

He shook his head. ''You know how it is. We're not always all at the same place at the same time. And anyway, whoever it is, he's probably only on the lookout. He makes a phone call, that's all. And someone else actually does the job.''

''Back in February, the sheriff came out and talked to all the hands, didn't he?''

''Yeah. They interviewed everyone here at the Rising Sun—and everyone working the nearby ranches. They came up with zip.''

''But maybe now that you've found tracks to match the ones from February, the sheriff will send someone out to do some more interviewing. Maybe this time they'll find out something that slipped by them back in February.''

''Tess. This time, I've got no real proof of anything. It's tire tracks and a bad feeling and that's about all.''

''Well, why else would those tracks be there, except that more cattle were stolen?''

''Good question. But I still wouldn't expect a lot of action from the sheriff's office. They need more to go on, and that's a plain fact.'' He sounded tired and discouraged. Tess wanted to reach out and put her hand over his, in a gesture of support and reassurance. But she stopped herself. It seemed a big step, a touch like that.

And they were doing so well. Why court rejection?

She kept her hands to herself and reasoned, ''Still, the brands would have to be inspected before the cattle could be sold, wouldn't they?''

He took a pull off the beer. ''Sure, though it's a real good possibility they're taking them somewhere and butchering them right off. But say they did sell them on the hoof. It's a damn sight easier to get away with an altered brand if you took the cow in Wyoming and you're selling her off in Chicago.'' He set the beer down and looked at it as if he couldn't figure out how the label had gotten peeled halfway off. ''I heard somewhere that there are over 57,000 brands registered today—in the state of Montana alone, I think it was. Multiply that by all the beef-producing states. They keep track of them by computer. They do what they can, but it's just not enough."

"It's a crime."

He let out a dry laugh. "Exactly."

Outside, the wind cried. Tess got up and put another log in the wood-burning side of the big kitchen stove. The Rising Sun had all the conveniences, including central propane heat. Still, they salvaged a lot of wood—from out in the pastures, from the edges of the juniper forests that grew up the mountains and from old, falling-down buildings. They used that wood for heat, sometimes hardly needing the propane at all.

Tess stared down for a moment, into the flames that burned in the belly of the stove. Behind her, Zach was silent and outside, the wind moaned. Tess watched the flames as they embraced the log she'd just fed them. The heat rose up, warming her face.

She heard Zach shift in his chair, and smiled. He was probably wondering what she found so interesting down inside the stove. She put the iron cover back in place and turned to find him watching her.

He said, "You did great today, when Jo fell off that horse. You didn't get nuts, the way some mothers would have."

"I felt pretty nuts."

"It's what you *did,* Tess. That's what counts. You're always a plus in a crisis."

She loved when he praised her. It made her feel so good inside. She dared to tease, "Always? How would you know?"

"I've watched. Remember the Christmas before last? When Abby got so sick?"

Just before Tyler Ross was born, Abby had fallen victim to eclampsia—extreme pregnancy-induced high blood pressure that had put her in a coma and almost killed her. They'd all been at the ranch, snowed in by a Christmas blizzard, when the condition became acute.

Zach made a musing sound in his throat. "We were all useless as udders on a bull—me, Nate, and especially Edna." He didn't mention Cash, who had been absolutely terrified for his wife, and had stuck right by her side, *willing* her to pull through. "But *you*," Zach said. "You called for the helicopter, and saw to making Abby as comfortable as possible. You dealt with Edna's near-hysterics. You kept your mind on what needed to be done, and you did it." He chuckled, shaking his head. "You were something that night."

Outside, the wind had died down for a moment. Tess, positively basking in such praise, whispered, "I was?"

Zach whispered back, "Yeah."

And they looked at each other, a long look, a look that drew on Tess somehow, pulling down into the center of her, making a warmth, a pooling sort of feeling. A feeling of...

Desire.

The word bloomed in her mind, as the warmth bloomed down inside her. Zach went on watching her, his eyes so steady, his whole lean body absolutely motionless, waiting...for what?

She wished he would move. She wished he would stand up and walk around the table and—

She cut off the thought. It seemed a wrong thought.

But why?

The answer came: because she loved Cash. She did. She had planned, as Zach's wife, to make love with Zach.

To be true to Zach in the ways that Zach demanded—in all ways, really, except deep in her most secret heart.

But to *want* Zach? To yearn for the feel of his hands on her skin, for the touch of his lips against her hair…

That hadn't been part of her plan at all.

Which was crazy. He was her husband. For her to want him should be very right.

Except that it called into question her love for Cash, made it seem a transitory thing. Made her affection seem cheap, that its focus could so easily shift.

Zach picked up his beer and drained the last of it, watching her the whole time.

In her belly, in spite of her shame, the hungry heat grew, rising up like the fire in the stove behind her, as if she'd somehow just given it fuel.

Zach set down the empty bottle, then gestured at hers. "You haven't finished your beer."

She couldn't stop staring into his eyes. "I'm not much of a beer drinker."

He made no polite reply to that, only continued to stare right back at her in that arousing, fathomless way.

The shocking heat inside her burned hotter still. At the same time, his remark had her feeling obligated to drink the beer she'd opened. She stepped forward, picked up the bottle and took a sip, using the action to break the seductive hold of his gaze. When she lowered the bottle, a tiny bit of foam got away from her and dribbled over the edge of her lower lip.

She lifted her hand, to wipe it away—and her gaze locked with his again. She brushed at her chin, feeling mesmerized, lost somewhere in that level gaze of his.

All at once, her imagination got away from her. She pictured herself leaning across the table, stretching toward him, yearning, seeking—until her mouth met his and she sighed in both triumph and surrender.

In her imagination, he didn't turn away. In her imagination, he tasted a little of beer and a lot of the wind outside, with a slight tang of sage and cedar. In her imagination, he kissed her with longing. He kissed her with heat—slow, radiant heat, as from a well-tended fire that burned so hot beneath a layer of protecting ash. A fire that would last the whole night.

More than the night, a hundred nights.

A lifetime of nights...

Chapter Eight

In the stove behind her, a log must have shifted. Tess heard a dropping, settling sound. Zach went on watching her.

And she knew that if she didn't do something to break this strange erotic spell that had suddenly got hold of her, she would do something else. Something like what she had just imagined.

She would reach for him. And not just because they were married. Not just for the sake of another sweet child to hold in her arms.

But for him. For the feel of him. For the things they might do alone in the dark. For the sake of the act itself.

With him.

Tess dragged in a breath and made herself speak. "I'll get you another beer." She tore her gaze from his—that was what it felt like: tearing. And she turned to the refrigerator.

"No."

Startled at the flat, harsh sound of his voice, she whirled back to him. Their gazes locked again. Something—an energy, a current?—went zipping back and forth between them.

"One's enough," he said, and he stood.

She watched him, watched his tall, lean body unfold from behind the table. And she told herself he couldn't know what she'd just been thinking. Her mind was her own. No man could see into it.

All he could know was what had actually happened. They'd talked, and not one word of that talk had concerned the question of intimacy between them. He'd finished his beer. He didn't want another. Now he would leave her for the night.

He would go to his room and she would go to hers, just as they'd been doing every night since their wedding night.

"I guess I…" Her voice came out all ragged, revealing more than she wanted him to know.

"You guess you *what?*" It sounded like some kind of challenge.

She wasn't taking any challenge. No way. He was the one who'd said they were taking it slow, and if he wanted to take it faster, he'd just have to say so. Directly.

She ordered some starch into her tone. "Nothing. I guess *nothing.*"

He gave her a distant, completely unreadable smile. "Well, all right. Good night, then."

She nodded. "Good night."

He left her. A few minutes later, she poured the rest of her beer down the drain and then climbed the stairs herself. She put on her nightgown and cleaned her face and her teeth and she got into bed.

Outside, the wind blew. It did sound like crying. It truly did.

She wished those moments hadn't happened—those moments when he'd looked at her and she'd imagined kissing him. Kissing him, and a whole lot more. Those moments had confused her, made her wonder if she really understood herself at all. And whether he'd guessed her thoughts or not, Zach had withdrawn from her afterward.

He was such a careful, wary man. She felt certain a lot of lonely nights would go by before he sought her out again.

But it didn't work out that way. The next night, he surprised her by coming to find her again, after all his work was done. He came, as the night before, bearing more wood. He stoked the fire, then asked, "How about a beer?"

She grinned in pure happiness. He *hadn't* stayed away from her, after all. She jumped from her chair. "I'll get you one."

"And one for you, too."

She made a face. "No, thanks. Maybe a cup of tea."

"Suit yourself."

They adjourned to the kitchen, choosing seats at the table just like the night before.

They talked of everyday things, which was just fine with Tess. They discussed which sections of fence needed mending and shook their heads over a prize bull that had got his hoof infected so bad, they had to have the town vet out to see him.

Then Zach said, "I want you to have something."

She waited, wondering what in the world he might mean, as he got up and left the room. He returned a few minutes later with a small pistol in a hip holster and a box of shells.

He slid the gun from the holster. "This is a .380 Colt. Simple and effective. A revolver with six shots." He flipped out the empty cylinder, spun it, then flipped it back in. "You know how to load and shoot?"

She nodded. "My father taught me. I wasn't much older than Jobeth. He took me out where I couldn't hit anything that mattered and set cans on logs for me. Believe it or not, I wasn't bad."

He reholstered the pistol and handed it to her, along with the box of shells. "Any time you go riding alone, load it and take it with you. It's useful against varmints— on four legs or otherwise."

She thought of the rustlers, who might or might not be making regular runs at the stock. If they really were out there, she wouldn't want to come up on them without a means of defending herself.

"Thank you, Zach." She set the weapon and the shells carefully on the end of the counter to take upstairs with her when she went to bed. "I suppose I couldn't talk you into having one more beer."

He grinned. "Sure you could. Just this once."

Tess poured more boiling water on her tea bag and Zach got a second longneck. They sat at the table again. Tess mentioned the paint job she thought the house needed. "I want to do both the inside and the outside. Inside, everything's looking a little gray. And outside, it's starting to peel."

Zach said, "Yeah. I suppose you're right. It has been a few years."

Tess wanted to do the work herself, inside at least.

But Zach said no. "We always use the Bartley brothers." Tess had heard of Brad and Chip Bartley. They'd been painting the buildings of local residents for the past thirty years. "They do a fine job and they don't fool around. Give them a call. They'll show up with all their samples and give great advice on colors and brands. Then they'll buy the paint, and do the job fast and right. All you'll have to do is work around them for a few days."

"But it would be cheaper if—"

Zach tipped his beer toward her. "I don't want cheap. I want it done right."

"I can do it right."

He shook his head, his expression bemused. "Oh, Tess. I know you can."

"So then, let me—"

"You've got plenty to do. You know it and I know it. Let the Bartleys paint the damn house. Please."

She looked down at her teacup. "Fine. Waste your money."

"Our money. And it won't be wasted."

She felt pleasure, a warm sensation all through her, that he would make a point of calling his money hers. She didn't agree with him. To her mind, she'd have no real share in what Zach owned for some time now. Not until she'd earned it with the labor of her hands. And not until she and Zach were truly man and wife.

Still, it meant a lot, that one little word: *ours*. The sound of it on his lips was like a gift.

"Tess. Say you'll call the Bartleys."

She looked across the table into his eyes. "I'll call the Bartleys."

"Good."

She went on outlining her plans. "I thought I'd get going on the inside of the house right away. And wait a while, till the end of June at least, when the weather should be more dependable, to try the outside."

"Sounds good. Call the Bartleys tomorrow, then."

"I will."

They talked a little more, and then he left her for the night. As she washed her teacup, she was smiling, thinking how well things seemed to be going between them lately.

Last night, it had been a little scary—when she'd turned from the fire and found the heat still burned inside her.

But tonight, it had been only good talk. And sharing.

Still smiling, she put her teacup in the cupboard and picked up the Colt and shells to put them safely away. Another few nights like this, and she would actually start thinking they were making progress toward true closeness to each other.

The next day, Tess called the Bartley brothers. And by the end of the week, they were painting the upstairs bedrooms. By the start of the following week, they'd progressed to the downstairs rooms, beginning with the formal living room and the dining room. The end of that week, the last week in May, was the toughest. The Bartleys took over the kitchen and the great room. Tess served meals in the foreman's cottage for two days—and didn't mind the inconvenience at all.

Cheerfully she stepped over drop cloths and skirted paint cans. With the Bartleys' help, she'd chosen colors that seemed to lighten and brighten the rooms—pale blues and butter yellows, warm mauves and cloud grays. It gave her a great feeling of contentment, to see that summery freshness taking over the rooms that to her had always seemed just a little too musty and dim.

And things between her and Zach were going so well. He came to sit with her every night now before bed. They talked over the day just passed, they laughed together.

They spoke of Jobeth and how bravely she seemed to be bearing up under the deprivation of not being able to ride.

"Still, she's counting the days until we visit that doctor in Buffalo again," Tess said.

Zach chuckled. "Counting the hours, is more like it."

"Counting the minutes…"

"The seconds. And one thing's for sure. Callabash is the best groomed horse in Johnson County." Since Jobeth couldn't ride the horse, she spent what seemed like half of every afternoon brushing his hide until it shone like glass.

More suspicious tire tracks appeared in a pasture that shared a boundary with the Double-K. Beau and Lolly spotted them while out mending fences. Zach called the sheriff's office and the range detective came out, took pictures and asked questions. The next day the detective called back. He said the tire tracks matched the ones from the previous incidents, including the known thievery back in February. Then he went out and interviewed everyone over at the Double-K. Nate said they'd seen no evidence of rustling there, but they'd keep an eye out.

Zach and Tess discussed the grim situation a little more that night, at the kitchen table, over a pair of grape sodas.

"These guys are bound to get caught sooner or later," Tess predicted. "Someone will see them on Rising Sun land, or you or one of the hands will actually catch them in the act."

Zach shook his head. "We're talking roughly a hundred square miles of pastureland, Tess. And rustlers who know where and when to make a run at the stock. I just don't know. As long as they're careful and they don't get too greedy, this could go on for years."

"Oh, I hate to think that's possible."

"Sometimes the truth is not a pleasant thing." He

drank from his soda and when he set the can down, he
looked at her in that steady way he had—a level, measuring look that seemed to arouse her with its very directness.
But then, after no more than a second or two, he glanced
away.

Tess dropped her own gaze, feeling totally off balance,
half-relieved and half-disappointed, wondering if he
would ever make love to her, afraid that if he did, she
might like it more than she ought to for a woman whose
secret heart belonged to someone else.

When he looked back at her, he was smiling—a
friendly, teasing smile. He asked how she was holding up
with the Bartleys underfoot all the time.

She said, "They're doing a great job. And I'm holding
up just fine."

In the first week of June, after the Bartleys had packed
up their paintbrushes and cleared out until the end of the
month when they'd be back to do the exterior of the
house, Edna called with a hesitant but heartfelt request.

"I am just plain lonely, Tess. Isn't that silly?"

"No," Tess said firmly, knowing what was coming,
wishing she could feel happier about it than she did. "It's
not silly at all."

"I always thought I would love living alone. But I
don't. I want family around me. Of course, Abigail and
Cash have offered me a place with them. But they're gone
so much. And I love my daughter dearly, but you know
how we are with each other. I'd have her climbing the
walls in a week. And she'd get me so crazy, I'd end up
having to move out again."

Tess made an understanding sound in her throat. She'd
seen Abby and Edna together a lot, seen the strength of
their love and regard for each other—and also witnessed

the way each always managed to say exactly the thing that would set the other on edge.

Edna went on, "However, for some reason, you and I always seem to rub along just fine together. You're patient with my tendency to tell everyone what to do. You're patient with *me*. And I miss you. I miss Jobeth."

Tess listened with half an ear, her mind on the separate beds she and Zach slept in, the separate beds that Jobeth, at eight, didn't see as particularly odd. The separate beds that no one else knew about.

But if Edna moved in, then Edna would figure it out. And Tess didn't want her to know. She didn't want Edna looking at her with worry in her eyes. And she most certainly did not want to answer any of the questions that Edna would eventually work up the courage to ask.

"Well, anyway," Edna said briskly, "I've been thinking about the foreman's cottage. It's empty now, isn't it?"

The foreman's cottage. Across the yard. Tess breathed a little easier. If Edna wanted to live *there,* then Tess and Zach's privacy on the matter of their current sleeping arrangements just might be maintained.

Edna sighed. "Oh, no. I shouldn't have asked, should I? I can tell by your silence that it simply isn't a good idea."

Tess smiled into the phone. "Oh, really? I haven't said a word, and already you're sure I'm saying no?"

Edna made a small sound of distress. "Don't tease me. You know I hate to be teased."

"All right," Tess replied more gently. "I won't tease you. When will you move in?"

There was silence, then some sputtering. "Oh, really. Let's slow down a little here. You'll have to talk with Zach."

"Edna, you are always welcome here. We both know that."

"All the same, I would insist that you talk with Zach. Maybe he doesn't want an old lady around, getting in the way all time."

"Edna. Stop it. The Rising Sun is your home anytime you want to return to it. We all know it. Zach will only ask what I'm asking, which is when do you want to move in?"

"Soon." Edna's voice sounded so small, suddenly. "Right away."

"Then we'll move you. Right away."

"Talk to Zach. And call me back."

"Edna, it's not necessary."

"You will talk to him first. And then you will call me." Now the older woman's tone would have done Queen Victoria proud.

"All right. I'll talk to him tonight. And call you first thing in the morning."

The night was mild. Tess sat out on the long gallery at the front of the house, a light sweater across her shoulders and Zach's sweet old mutt, Reggie, on the step beside her. Maybe she was testing Zach a little, seeing if he'd come all the way out to the porch to find her.

When she heard the door open behind her, she smiled. He had come. He had made the extra effort to seek her out in a different place. It was a small thing. But small things added up.

He came and stood over her. "What are you up to?"

She leaned her head back a little. "Watching the clouds float by that sliver of moon."

He made a small clicking noise with his tongue. With

a heavy sigh, old Reggie dragged himself off the step and stretched out on the ground below.

Zach sat in the dog's place. For a moment, they were silent, staring out at the night together. A coyote howled, off near the mountains.

Then Tess spoke softly. "It's a nice night. Almost warm."

"It is at that."

She turned and looked at him. He was watching her. It was one of those moments, when his eyes said things his lips never did. In those eyes she saw promises. Pleasures. Fulfillment.

A shiver went through her. She gathered her sweater a little tighter, wondering, If I scooted over close to him, pressed myself shamelessly against him, would he put his arm around me?

"Cold?"

She should say yes, she should sidle on over like a cat seeking strokes. But her nerve failed her. "No, no. I'm fine."

He looked out toward the night again and the moment passed, leaving her a little let down, a little edgy. A little bit hungry for what might have been.

She remembered her conversation with Edna. "Zach?"

He looked at her again, cocking an eyebrow.

"Edna called today."

He went on looking at her for a long moment, then he said, "She wants to move back out here, to the ranch."

She stared at him. "How did you know?"

He shrugged. "Edna's more a mother to me than Elaine Bravo ever was. I know her. She was in heaven, in town, when you and Jo were there with her. But she's got to be lonely, all by herself. She needs people she cares for close by, to coddle. And to boss around." He reached out, tugged on the edge of her sweater. "You knew she'd be coming eventually. Didn't you?"

Tess felt breathless and lovely. That little tug on her sweater had almost been a caress.

"Tess. Didn't you know?"

"Yes. Yes, I did."

"Does she want her old room back?" Edna's old room was the room he slept in now; a nice, large, west-facing room with its own private bath. What would he have done, if Edna did want it back? Move to the one room that was left, and share a bath with Jobeth?

Oh, she didn't understand him. He seemed totally unconcerned about what Edna might discover if she lived in the house with them.

"Tess." He was looking at her sideways. "Did you hear my question?"

"Oh. Sorry. No, not her old room. She asked about the foreman's cottage."

He seemed to consider that, then nodded. "That's a good idea. She'd be close to us, but she'd have her privacy."

And so would we, Tess thought but didn't say. "Yes. It is. A good idea."

"When's she coming?"

"I take it that means you have no problem with her moving here."

His brows drew together in a puzzled frown. "How could I have a problem? She's Edna. She's always got a place here."

"That's exactly what I told her, but she kept insisting that I had to ask you first, before we agreed on the move."

He grunted, a sound of bafflement. "She's funny."

"She doesn't want to intrude."

"Intrude on what?" He was looking at her again, steadily. Probingly.

She just looked right back at him, saying nothing.

"Intrude on what, Tess?"

She felt angry with him, suddenly. For the way he could affect her lately, for this new and bewildering power he seemed to wield over her senses. And for his ability to hide whatever was going on inside him—if there actually *was* anything going on inside him.

She squared her shoulders and replied tartly, "She doesn't want to intrude on us, on our lives together as...man and wife."

He regarded her, taking his time as he always did, before he spoke again. Then he said, "She won't intrude, not as far as I'm concerned. What about you?"

She wanted to throw back her head and howl at that sliver of moon up above. Howl in frustration. In confusion. In pure aggravation. But she didn't. Oh, no. She could be every bit as calm and collected as he could, yessiree.

"No, Zach," she said, with excruciating sweetness. "It's not a problem for me. Not at all. Not one bit. I mean, why should it be? What's there to *intrude* on, anyway?"

Did he tense up, just a little? Had she gotten to him, just a tiny bit? She hoped so. It was small and petty and mean of her, but she did hope so. She hoped that he—

Her vindictive thoughts flew right out of her head as he reached for her. His hand—so warm, so rough, so exactly what she craved—slid around to cup her nape.

He pulled her to him, slowly. And when their lips were inches apart, he whispered, "What's your problem?"

His hand moved, at her nape, his fingers threading themselves into her hair. It felt good, so right, to have him touch her....

"Tess." He said her name in a whisper. "What is your problem?"

She made herself whisper right back at him, calmly, with assurance, "I don't know what you mean," as if he wasn't so close. Or as if he got that close all the time. "I don't have any problem."

He lowered his gaze to watch her mouth move, and then he met her eyes again. Almost tenderly, he murmured, "Good, then. Tell her to move in. Right away."

She whispered back, all sweetness, "That's exactly what I'll tell her."

And he said, "Fine."

And she said, "It's settled then."

"Yeah," he muttered. "Settled."

And then he moved forward, just a fraction, until his lips brushed hers—so lightly, hardly more than a touch. Enough to make her yearn for more.

Almost instantly, he released her and stood.

She looked up at him, not trusting herself to speak.

He was already turning away, for the front door. "Good night." He tossed the words back at her, over a shoulder, then opened the door and went inside.

Once he was gone, she sat for a long time, watching the night, listening to a lone dove somewhere over near the foreman's cottage as it cooed forlornly in the dark.

Chapter Nine

Edna moved into the foreman's cottage that Saturday. Cash wanted to hire a regular moving company, but Edna wouldn't hear of such an expense. So they rented a moving truck to transport the furniture. Zach and Cash provided the muscle.

By evening, they had it all moved in. Then Cash, Abby and Tyler Ross stayed for dinner. Tess served pork tenderloins and green beans and mashed potatoes with pork gravy. The food was great, as usual. Zach looked at his wife down the table. She glanced up and smiled at him. As he smiled in return, he realized how good it made him feel to see her there. Real good. Maybe too good.

Cash made some offhand remark. Everyone laughed. Zach watched his wife as she laughed, too, a thoroughly appropriate laugh, neither too warm nor too long. She hid her feelings well. No one would guess how she felt about Cash.

No one but her husband, who just happened to have caught her at an unguarded moment, when her heart showed in her eyes.

After the meal, the women, along with Jobeth and Tyler Ross, retreated to the foreman's cottage.

Zach turned to Cash. "Come on. Let's have a look at the books."

Cash immediately tried to get out of it. "Zach. Give it a rest. I've been lugging Edna's damn furniture around all afternoon. I'd like another drink. And I'd really like a smoke."

"You quit."

"Don't remind me. Let's just go in the other room and get the bottle of Black Jack from the cabinet and—"

"Get the bottle. And bring it in my office."

Cash tried a stubborn glare. "Zach."

"You and Nate have to know what goes on around here."

"We do know. You're the operator and a damn fine one and when I'm curious about the bottom line, I'll let you know."

"Go get the bottle. And a couple of glasses. And come on."

Cash moaned and groaned some more, but he finally got the whiskey and glasses and followed Zach into the office.

They sat together at the computer and Zach scrolled through the spreadsheets, showing his cousin exactly how the ranch was doing in terms of dollars and cents.

"The count seems a little low," Cash said, referring to the number of cattle they'd counted during branding time just passed. "It's not all that bad, but it's just not quite up to what we thought it would be."

"No, it's not." With a frustration that made a burning

in his gut, Zach thought of the mysterious tire tracks that kept appearing in his pastures. Cash knew all about the tracks. Zach kept both him and Nate posted on the situation.

"Come on," Cash said. "Don't look so damn grim. These numbers tell me we're absorbing the loss with no problem—if there really is a loss."

"There's a loss, bet on it. The tracks we found in February match the ones we've found since then. We're getting hit. And regularly. And if—*when*—I catch those bastards, there will be hell to pay."

Cash chuckled. "You're starting to get mad, cousin."

"That I am."

"But you *never* get mad."

"Never say never."

Cash looked at Zach for a long moment, then slowly shook his head. "I pity those poor S.O.B.'s—" he smiled that smile that drove the women wild "—*when* you find them." He frowned, then grinned again. "Hey. I almost forgot."

"What?"

"Wait right there." Cash got up and went out through the dining room.

Zach exited the spreadsheet program, switched off his computer and waited. His cousin returned a few minutes later, carrying a box.

"What now?" Zach asked grimly.

Cash was beaming. He pulled a cell phone from the box, a big one, about the size of an appointment book. "Your very own cellular phone. A bag phone, in this case. Three watts of pure power. That's enough to get pretty good reception anywhere on the Rising Sun. And don't give me that what-a-waste-of-money look. These things are damn convenient. You break your leg—or run into our phantom rustlers—out in the North Pasture, you'll be glad you can just phone home.'' He grunted. '''Course, cell phones have a drawback or two. Sometimes the reception's not so great on them—especially around these parts, even with a bag phone. Also if you don't recharge them, they go dead.''

"And a call on one costs a fortune.''

"Don't be a skinflint. You need to keep up with the times. This baby's all set up and ready to go. Let me show you how it works.''

"You mean the Rising Sun will be getting a bill any day now.''

"Come on, come on. You're gonna love this....''

A few minutes later, Zach set down his new cell phone. ''Thanks.''

"You're welcome. Before you know it, you'll be wanting them for Tess and Edna, too.''

"We'll see.'' Zach shot Cash a sideways look. ''Got a smoke?''

Cash raked a hand back through his gold hair. ''You just said it an hour ago. I quit.''

Zach grunted. ''Yeah. But have you got a cigarette?''

Cash studied Zach as if he were some strange new species of man. ''How long's it been, since you had a smoke?''

Zach drained the last of his whiskey. ''Six months, a year. I couldn't say for sure.''

"Haven't you heard? Smoking's addictive.''

"I can take it or leave it.''

"Right. Rub it in.''

Zach set down his empty glass. ''You didn't answer my original question.''

Cash sent a furtive glance toward the door to the dining room, as if he expected Abby to come strolling through it the minute he lit up. Then he lowered his voice. "We could go out back, by the barn."

Zach grinned. "Yeah, that's a long way from the foreman's cottage, where your wife is right now."

Cash said, "Don't even give me that smirky-assed look. Abby worries about me, that's all. She cares about my health."

"Abby's right," Zach said, feeling bad all of a sudden, wondering where the hell his own good judgment had gone. Though Nate had quit years ago and Zach rarely smoked, Cash struggled constantly with a nicotine addiction that he never seemed to lick. Zach had no business suggesting that the two of them light up. "Forget I asked about it."

Cash laughed. "It's too late to forget now."

"No, it's not."

"It just so happens I've got a pack stashed in the moving truck."

"Look. I said let it go."

Cash peered at Zach more closely. "Something bothering you, cousin?"

Zach kept his face expressionless, though Tess's image flashed through his mind. "No. Why?"

"You seem edgy tonight. And you're always the upright one. It's not like you to even mention a cigarette around a nicotine fiend like me."

Zach figured extended denials would only make his cousin more suspicious. "Maybe I am a little on edge. It's the missing stock, I guess."

"Well," Cash said. "If you've changed your mind about that smoke, good for you. I haven't."

Zach turned for the door. "Fine. Go get the damn things. I'll meet you out back."

They hung on the fence to the horse pasture, the smoke from their cigarettes trailing up toward the stars. Callabash and Ladybird trotted over, accepted a little coddling, and then wandered away.

"So how's married life treatin' you?" Cash asked after they'd puffed away for a few minutes in silence.

Zach shot his cousin a look. But Cash just went on smoking, totally oblivious to Zach's problems—or to his own perfectly innocent part in them.

Cash turned and squinted through the cloud of smoke. "Well?"

"Good," Zach said. "Real good."

"Tess is a fine woman."

"Yeah. She is."

"She deserved a real chance for once."

"She sure did."

"And because of you, she got it."

Zach looked away, out toward the center of the pasture, where Ladybird was nipping at the grass.

Cash added, "And the house looks great. The new paint really lightens things up."

Zach sucked in more acrid smoke and wondered what the hell had possessed him to ask for a cigarette, anyway. "Yeah. Tess chose all the colors. She has an eye for stuff like that."

Cash fell silent, then asked, "Are you sure you're all right?"

"I'm good, Cash. Real good." Other than the fact that some rustling bastard is stealing us blind and my wife's in love with you. "And we probably ought to be heading on back inside."

Cash made a noise of agreement as he crushed the butt under his heel.

Zach put out his own cigarette and started to turn for the house.

Cash said, "Hey."

Zach turned back. "Yeah?"

"Maybe we should hire some men. To patrol the place. What do you think?"

Zach considered, and then shook his head. "Let's give it a while. See if it keeps up."

"You think they'll stop?"

"No."

Cash was looking at him real hard. "You don't want them to stop."

"I did at first. But now…"

"You just want to catch them in the act."

"You got it."

"Be careful."

Zach let out a humorless laugh. "You know me, cousin. Careful is my middle name."

That night, after Cash and his family left for town and Jobeth had gone to bed, Tess sat out on the front porch step with Reggie. Across the yard, the lights were on in the foreman's cottage. Edna would be settling in for her first night in her new home.

Tess drew up her knees, smoothing the skirt she wore down over them. Reggie gave a little whine, so she scratched him behind one of his droopy ears.

Actually, the foreman's cottage wasn't new to Edna. It had been her home for years before she moved to the main house. That had been back when Ross Bravo, Zach's grandfather, had run the Rising Sun. Edna had lived in the cottage with her husband Ty, the Rising Sun's top hand. Tess had never met Ty. He had died just a few months before she and Jobeth had come to Medicine Creek.

Abby had been born in the foreman's cottage—during a blizzard when there'd been no way to get to the hospital in Buffalo. Cash, who was fifteen years old at the time, had been there when it happened. He had held Abby as a tiny baby, less than an hour after she first entered the world.

Tess smiled at the idea of a man holding his wife on the day of her birth. And then she frowned.

For some reason, right then, she found she was thinking of her father, dead now for several years. Roger Inman had been a tall, serious man—hardworking and kind. Even when he'd learned that his unmarried teenage daughter was pregnant, he hadn't raised a hand to her.

He'd only said, "It's time for truth, daughter. All of it, I think."

She had cried and told him about Josh. And he had listened, his eyes so sad and disappointed in her. But still kind. Still full of love.

He'd taken her out to the room off the barn where Josh slept. And Josh had looked so white and scared at first, but then he'd said he did love her. And would marry her.

So she had bound her life to him. That had been at the start of her senior year of high school. She'd been a straight-A student and she'd managed, just barely, to finish her required classes and graduate a semester early, before she got too big with Jobeth. At the time it hadn't occurred to her or her father—or Josh, either, for that matter—that there might have been some other choice besides marriage. She was seventeen and pregnant and needed a husband. Period.

Over in the foreman's cottage, the living room went

dark. A few seconds later, the front bedroom light came on. Edna would be getting ready for bed.

Time for truth, daughter, her father used to say. Time for truth.

Tess pulled her sweater a little closer around her shoulders and thought of Cash, of the moment this afternoon when he'd driven up in the moving truck with Abby and Tyler. Zach had followed behind them in the blue pickup, with Edna on the passenger side.

Tess had been over in the foreman's cottage, freshening things up a bit for Edna's arrival. She'd heard the vehicles and run out to the porch. She'd seen the moving truck—and realized that Zach wasn't in it.

So she'd looked toward the pickup, seeking the shadow of Zach's hat in the window. And when she'd seen it, seen his profile and his strong hands on the wheel, she'd felt that rising, joyful feeling that she used to get at the sight of Cash.

Tess closed her eyes, drew in a long breath of the cool night air and laid her cheek down on her drawn-up knees. She felt so bewildered. And lost. So out of sorts with the world and her knowledge of herself.

She wanted Zach. She yearned for his touch, for a kind word, for a smile across the table during dinner. For a kiss on the porch after dark…

Oh, it felt like love. Exactly like love.

And it made her feel foolish and shallow, a woman whose affections changed with each shift in the winds. It made her wonder if she'd ever understood love at all—and if she was capable of loving a good man the way such a man deserved to be loved, with steadiness and loyalty, for as long as they both should live.

Behind her, she heard the front door open. Zach. It would be Zach. She hadn't thought he would come to talk with her tonight. He hadn't sought her out for the past two nights. Not since Wednesday night, when he'd kissed her and then gone inside so swiftly, leaving her to wonder if he regretted that sweet brushing of his lips against hers.

She heard his step, behind her. And then he made the small clicking noise with his tongue that signaled Reggie. The dog got up and moved out of the way.

Zach dropped down beside her.

The warmth of his body reached out to her. She kept her gaze on the foreman's cottage. She watched the light in the bedroom go out, but she watched without really seeing. Her mind was filled with the man sitting beside her, her senses humming with gladness and anxiety at his nearness. She felt shy, suddenly, and feared turning to face him. So she didn't. She just sat there, staring into the night.

And as Tess looked at the night, Zach looked at her, his gaze tracing her soft profile, wondering what she was thinking—but not sure that he'd like what he heard if she told him.

On one level, this practical marriage had turned out to be exactly what he'd hoped it might. The hands went to work smiling, their bellies full of good food. The house his grandfather had built was a place of order and comfort. Tess filled the rooms with warmth and light.

Beyond the good she did in his home, she had brought him Jobeth, who would make one hell of a rancher someday. Every day Zach felt more and more certain that there would be someone to take the reins from him when the time came to pass them on.

Things had worked out just as he'd hoped.

Except for the wanting. The wanting was the problem.

He wanted Tess too much. And he wanted her more and more all the time. He probably shouldn't have come out here tonight. But she drew him. He'd known she was out here. And he just couldn't stay away.

The thought came all the time now, that she was his wife and he had a right to her body. That she would accept him willingly in her bed, because she did want children, after all. That she was only waiting for him to reach out his hand.

It was damn scary. He felt so vulnerable to her. And he didn't want to be vulnerable. He just plain didn't need any woman having that kind of power over him—especially not Tess. Not Tess, his wife, who was absolutely perfect in every single way—except for the little problem that she loved another man.

She moved, turning her head slowly, seeking his eyes through the night. "I think it should work out just fine, with Edna in the foreman's cottage."

He looked at her, at her pretty, cat-slanted dark eyes and her smooth brow and that mouth with its neat little bow at the top. Her mouth drove him crazy, it was so soft and sweet.

She frowned. "Zach. Don't you think so?"

"What?"

"That Edna's going to be fine, living in the—"

"Oh. Edna. Yeah. Edna's fine."

"Are you...all right?"

"I'm fine."

She let out a little sigh and hugged her knees up close to her chest so she could rest her chin on them. He thought of leaning over, putting his mouth against her neck, sucking a little, making a mark there. Then kissing that mark. Of pulling her to him, opening her shirt, seeing her breasts, in the moonlight, touching them, kissing them. Then taking her hand, leading her in the house and up the stairs...

She laid her head sideways on her knees, so she could look at him. "What is it?"

"Nothing."

"You seem so…"

"What?"

"I don't know…" She waited, probably for him to supply some explanation of his mood. He supplied nothing, so she sighed again and lifted her head to look out at the yard. He watched her lips curve as she smiled. "Jobeth was so sweet tonight, keeping Tyler Ross out of trouble while Abby and I helped Edna unpack." She closed her eyes, tipped her head up, as if she were offering her pretty face to the night. "One more week, and she can go back to the doctor. Maybe, if she's lucky, that cast can come off."

"Yeah."

She looked at him again. God, he could smell her, smell the special scent of her body, so warm and sweet and tempting.

Somewhere around the time he'd imagined sucking a red mark onto her neck, he'd become hard. A damn humiliation if there ever was one. If he stood and she looked at the front of his Wranglers, she would know.

He was out of control. Completely out of control.

She looked away again, and smiled out at the night. "Tyler Ross is so cute. And it's funny, even though he's hardly more than a baby, he's got that Bravo look stamped on him so strong."

He watched her mouth. Watched that dreamy smile. And he knew she had to be thinking about Cash.

"What do you mean, that Bravo look?" It came out harsh, full of challenge, angry-sounding.

She snapped her head around. "What is wrong?"

He ached, that was what. For her. For her soft body.

All around him. For the release that sinking into her tender flesh would bring. "Nothing. I just asked what you meant. What *Bravo* look?"

Her gaze scanned his face, lighting briefly on his mouth. "Well, the mouth."

"The mouth?"

"Kind of full, for a man. And the nose. A very strong nose. And the eyes…I don't know. It's just…the way you all look."

She kept smiling, and he knew, though it was dark, that her skin was flushed. He would feel the heat, if he touched her.

God. He wanted to touch her. To reach out and—

"Look," he said gruffly.

"What?"

"I'm going in." He stood, quickly, and turned away before she could see the proof of the power she had over him.

"But, Zach—"

"Good night." He headed for the door.

He heard her jump to her feet and start coming for him. "Wait. What's the matter?"

"Nothing's the matter."

"That's not true. What did I do?"

He reached for the door. "Nothing."

She caught up with him. He could feel her, at his back. And then she made the mistake of putting her hand on his shoulder. "Zach—"

It was too much, that soft touch, that pleading tone. He spun on her and reached out, grabbed her by the hips and yanked her tight against him.

"Oh!" Those cat eyes went wide as she felt it, felt what she did to him.

"You happy?" he snarled, pulling her tighter still, feeling the heat of her, starving for more.

"I didn't... Oh, Zach..." No more words came.

And that was fine with him. He didn't want any words anyway. He could put that mouth of hers to use just fine doing other things than talking.

He lowered his head and took that mouth. It gave beneath his, parting, sighing, welcoming him. He ground his hips against hers, holding her tight, almost hoping she would refuse him, push him away.

But she didn't. She surged up with a small cry, and twined her slim arms around his neck. He felt her, the whole slender, sighing length of her. Her breasts pressed against his chest, so soft and round and full. And her hips—her hips pushed right back at him, answering, beckoning, welcoming him.

He bit her lower lip, not too hard, just enough to let her know that he might hurt her, might be rough with her, the need was so strong in him right then. She whimpered, a sound of surrender, a sound that said he could do what he wanted with her. He twined his hands in her silky hair, pulling a little, tipping her head back. And his mouth slid down, over the curve of her chin, to her neck. He licked the smooth, warm flesh and then he sucked, as he had imagined doing, putting his teeth against the skin, bringing a welt that would leave a slight bruise by morning. She clasped his head, holding him to her, as if she craved that mark.

He wanted to see her. All of her. To take her clothes away from her and have the whole of her body, all of her. For himself.

He froze.

And in spite of the roaring of his blood, the hunger in his body, he remembered.

He would not have her. Not *all* of her.

She tipped her hips against him, tried to tempt him to take her mouth again, to make him forget that what she offered wasn't everything. Wasn't complete.

"Oh, Zach…"

"No."

"Don't pull away. Please—"

He took her shoulders and very deliberately held her away from him. His body throbbed at the loss of a heaven not quite attained.

"Zach—"

"No, I said. No." He took his right hand from her shoulder and put it across those soft, tempting lips. "Listen."

She looked at him, waiting, her eyes begging with him over the mask of his hand. He dragged in a breath. "You'll listen?"

She nodded.

He said in a ragged whisper, "I loved my first wife. She cut out my heart and used it for buzzard bait. I don't need that again."

She pushed his hand away from her mouth. "I would never—"

He squeezed her shoulder. "Let me finish."

She swallowed. "All right."

He released her, stepping back. She swayed on her feet a little when he let go. But then she collected herself, drew in a breath and stood tall.

He chose his words with great care. "This is a good marriage we have. A practical one. One that's working out fine for both of us. I say we don't mess it up."

She made a small, frustrated noise. "But how could we mess it up by doing…what married people do?"

He stared at her for a long, deep moment, knowing that

she wouldn't like hearing the truth any more than he wanted to say it.

"Zach. Please. Tell me, talk to me..."

So he did.

"I know who's in your heart, Tess. And it's not me."

Chapter Ten

Tess gave a cry and put her hand against her mouth. Her eyes went wide and wounded. She couldn't have looked more shocked if he had slapped her hard across the face.

For a long, gruesome moment, they stared at each other. Then she dropped her hand. She whispered raggedly, "How did you know?"

Zach had a sinking, weary feeling, then. Until that moment, somewhere deep inside him, he had hoped that just maybe he'd been mistaken about this.

Her lower lip trembled. "It was that night, wasn't it? The night we moved our things out here. The night of the engagement party. You came up the basement stairs and you..." She seemed unable to finish.

So he finished for her. "I saw the look you gave Cash."

She wrapped her arms around herself and murmured numbly, "I thought so. But I didn't want to believe it. And then, when you didn't say anything..." She closed her eyes, drew in a breath and then looked at him once more. "So. That means, on our wedding night, it wasn't just time you were talking about. It was…what you knew. You didn't want me, because of what you knew." She started shaking her head, her face pale as death through the shadows on the porch.

He took a step toward her. "Tess—"

She backed up, still shaking her head. "You don't understand. Nobody knows. Nobody was ever going to know.…"

"Well. *I* know."

"Oh, dear Lord." She turned away, went to the porch rail, looked out across the yard again, into darkness, into someplace he couldn't see.

He said, "I guess I've made a mistake, to come looking for you in the evenings, to think we could make more of this marriage than it is."

She said nothing. Her slim back was very straight.

He spoke again. "Look. I meant what I said. We have a good thing. A practical arrangement. I think we should just keep it that way."

Still, she didn't speak, only wrapped an arm around the pillar next to her and leaned her cheek against it. He felt alarm, then. Concern for her.

"Tess. Are you all right?"

She waved the hand that wasn't wrapped around the pillar. "Fine. Just…it's hard to think that all this time, you've known. But I'll be okay. Really."

He pushed his concern for her aside. After all, she said she would be okay.

And he wanted to get a few things settled. His desire had died with her admission that she loved his cousin. He wanted it to stay dead. He wanted things back on an even keel. He wanted an understanding between them. And he wanted distance.

"Are you agreed, then? We'll keep things as they are. We won't go…stirring things up." He waited for her reply. When none came, he prompted, "Well?"

She seemed to shake herself. "Yes. Of course. Whatever you say."

"Good." As he said the word, he found he hated it. It wasn't good. Not good at all. But they would manage. It would be…bearable. She would take care of him and the hands and the house. And he would provide for her and Jobeth.

They'd treat each other with respect and civility. And they'd keep clear of each other in any personal sense.

She seemed awfully quiet. He said, "Are you sure you're all right?"

She didn't answer for a moment. He almost asked again. But then she let out a deep sigh. "I'm fine, Zach. And I'd like to be alone now, please."

She looked so lonely, standing there, staring into nothingness. Just about as lonely as he felt. He lifted his hand, to touch her, to reassure her.

But then he dropped it. Distance. That was what they'd agreed on. And she'd just asked him to leave her alone.

He said, "Good night, then."

And she replied, "Yes. Good night."

Once Zach left, Tess waited long enough for him to get all the way to his room. Then, moving very carefully because her silly legs felt so wobbly, she turned and went inside. She had to keep a firm grip on the bannister all the way up to the second floor.

And when she lay down between the cool sheets, she didn't close her eyes. She stared into the darkness, hearing

Zach's awful words in her mind, over and over and over again.

I know who's in your heart, Tess.

She had always taken such comfort from the belief that not a soul had guessed her feelings for Cash. But Zach knew. He had known since before he married her.

The shame…it was burning all through her. So much worse, to think that Zach knew.

He knew. And he had married her anyway.

Because he thought they could make a good life together, whatever she felt in her foolish heart.

He had married her anyway.

Because, as he'd made so clear from the first, he didn't need or want her love.

With a small moan, she turned on her left side, then tossed to her right. But sleep didn't come for her.

She kept reliving that moment when he had told her that he knew.

And she wondered why she hadn't answered, Yes, Zach. It's true. I did think I loved Cash. For years, I thought I loved him. But now, Lord help me, I think that I love you.…

Tess sat up in bed. And then she flopped back down.

Of course, she hadn't said such a thing. And she was glad that she hadn't. Because he never would have believed it. Hearing it in her mind, *she* didn't even believe it. It sounded so silly and impossible. It sounded like a desperate and pitiful lie, the kind of thing some low woman with no dignity would say to try to get a man to trust her.

Tess rolled to her stomach. She closed her eyes and wondered how she would face him, how she would live with him, day to day, knowing that he knew.

Should she leave? Just pack up Jobeth and their few

things and go? She had about a thousand dollars in her old checking account, money she had earned working for Carmen Amestoy. She could manage on that, somehow, until she found a job—as long as she found a job fast.

She thought of Jobeth, of how she had changed since they'd moved here. Jobeth had pride now, in her new life and in her place within it. Jobeth adored Zach. If she took Jobeth away from here, it would break her heart.

Oh, Lord. She didn't want to do that to Jobeth. Not if she could help it.

Time, Zach had said on their wedding night, when he had already known her secret, but hadn't told her so. *Give it time.*

Yes. That was good advice, now as well as then. She was too full of shame and confusion to make any big decisions now, anyway. For a week or two at least, she wouldn't do anything at all. Except get by. Go through the motions. Do what needed to be done, day by day.

Zach had made it clear he still wanted her to care for his house, to put the meals on the table for the hands. And she loved it here. She did. She loved this life just as much as her daughter did.

Yes. She would give it time. She would face Zach in the morning with a smile. And she would get through the days, one hour at a time.

Tess turned on her back again. She stared at the ceiling.

She longed for morning, when she could rise and work hard and try to forget what had happened tonight.

In the morning, when she washed her face, Tess saw the red mark on her neck where Zach had kissed her. She blushed all over, remembering. And the blush deepened as she realized that everyone would see it and guess how she'd acquired it.

Under the circumstances, she could almost laugh. That little red love bite lied. Oh, how it lied.

She put makeup on the mark and buttoned her collar all the way to the top. But the mark would still be visible to anyone who looked hard enough.

At breakfast, Zach treated her kindly. He complimented her biscuits and took seconds on bacon. Once or twice, she caught him looking at her neck.

Well, fine. Let him look. He had put that love bite there himself, after all.

He finished his meal a little faster than usual and then he went out with Tim to check the mineral tubs in a pasture not far from the house, reminding her before he left to be ready for church on time.

Edna stared after him, beaming from ear to ear. "I am just so glad you and Zach found each other." She picked up her plate and began helping Tess load the dishwasher.

Tess rinsed glassware at the sink and tried to look glad, too.

"You were just…meant for each other."

Tess set the glasses in the top rack of the dishwasher. "Yes. We have the same interests."

"Oh, it's much more than that. Any fool can see, by the way he looks at you, that he loves you deeply. And of course, I know you feel the same way for him."

"Yes. I do. I…love him very much." Strange. When she said it, it sounded right. It sounded true.

"It's amazing, I never believed he'd find happiness again." Edna lowered her voice to a conspiratorial whisper. "After Leila, you know."

"Yes. Yes, I know."

"But it's worked out perfectly, between you, hasn't it?"

"Yes, Edna. Perfectly."

Zach came in right on time, cleaned up and took them to church. He sat beside Tess in the pew, a model husband, sharing a hymnal with her, his deep voice steady and sure when they sang. Once or twice, his arm brushed hers, when they rose and when they sat down again. He was so close. And yet he might as well have been a thousand miles away.

Tess noticed, as one day faded into the next, that Zach found a lot of work to do far away from the house. He avoided coming in for the substantial midday meal she always served. She saw him at breakfast and dinner, when he treated her gently, if somewhat distantly.

He never came near her when his day's work was through.

For the first couple of nights, that was just fine with her. At first, every time she looked at him, all she thought of was her secret. Her secret that he knew. But as the days passed, and she got used to the idea that he knew, she found that she missed him. Missed their evenings together, missed the sound of his voice as he talked about his day, missed his wry smiles and his occasional, unpracticed laughter. Heaven help her, she even missed the agony of wondering if, maybe, *this* was the night he would truly make her his.

She began to understand the real reason she hadn't packed up her belongings and taken her daughter away. She began to see that she wasn't through with Zach Bravo yet. Not by a long shot. And, whether he was willing to admit it or not, he wasn't through with her.

He could say that all he wanted was a housekeeper and a cook. But he'd signed on for a wife. And by golly, in the end, she would do all in her power to see that he got one.

She began watching him, covertly, every chance she

got. And she saw the way he looked at her when he thought she didn't see, saw it much more clearly than she had before, when she'd been confused about her own feelings, and so jealously guarding her secret.

He did want her.

If she had any doubt about that, all she had to do was think of the way he had kissed her the other night, the way he had pulled her so hard against him—so she would know exactly how he felt. The mark on her neck had faded quickly, but not the memory of the way he had put it there.

As a claim. A brand.

There was a lot of passion behind Zach Bravo's impassive facade—if a woman just had the patience and stamina to pry him open and let it loose.

Shamelessly she pumped Edna for information. In the late mornings, after the breakfast things were cleared and she'd put in an hour on the house and an hour or two in her garden, she'd just wander on over to the foreman's cottage, where she knew Edna would have the coffee on.

They'd share a cup. And Tess would ask Edna things about Zach, about what he'd been like as a boy.

"A lot like he is now," Edna said. "Serious. Cautious. Honest. Upright. He used to drive Cash and Nate crazy. They both had the devil in them. And he was such a good boy. Yet they both wanted his respect. When either one of them would act up, all Zach would have to do was look at them with that direct, uncompromising stare of his. You know what I mean."

"Oh, I do. I do."

"Zach would give them a look. And they'd straighten up—or at least they'd feel good and guilty about whatever trouble they were up to. And that would mean that, soon enough, they'd stop."

Tess asked about Leila. "Tell me. What was she *like?*"

Edna frowned, thinking about Zach's first wife, and then she sighed. "Leila Wickerston had black hair and big blue eyes." Edna laughed. "What am I saying? I'm sure Leila still has black hair and blue eyes. It isn't as if she's passed on or anything. She's down there in San Diego with that rich second husband of hers and that little hellion, Starr."

"But what was she like, Edna? When she and Zach were together?"

"Beautiful. Spoiled, I suppose. All the boys were after her. But she only wanted Zach. And Zach, well, you know how he is."

"Of course, but tell me anyway."

"He tried to fight it at first. Even as a boy, he gave his heart…carefully. Does that make sense?"

"Yes. Yes, it does."

"We all used to laugh, about the way Leila was always finding ways to put herself where he was. He was active in 4-H. And all of a sudden, Leila was raising chickens. The Wickerstons lived in town, so they had no room for big animals. But Leila got those chickens. Skinniest birds you ever saw. She didn't pay much attention to them, you see. They were only a means to an end."

"The end being Zach."

"Precisely. Of course, Zach saw how she treated those birds and he said he wouldn't have anything to do with her. She'd never make a ranch wife. But Leila had other tricks."

"Like what?"

"Well, you know how Zach is. Church every Sunday. Not like Cash and Nate, both of whom I used to have to drag there. Zach's not terribly religious, but he believes in showing respect to the Lord on a regular basis. The

Wickerstons were strictly Christmas and Easter church-goers. But once Leila decided she wanted Zach, all of a sudden, that girl got religion. She always showed up in the same pew we sat in, waving and smiling and looking so sweet. She joined the Methodist Youth Fellowship and she bullied Zach until he joined, too. And then, naturally, he had to stop by her house to pick her up for the meetings. It took her about a year of constantly being everywhere Zach was.''

"And then?"

"Well, and then he surrendered."

Tess wrinkled her nose at that. "He *surrendered?*"

"I don't know what else to call it. He just…gave in and decided to love her. And when he did, he was so…devoted. It was lovely, really. And on her behalf, I'd have to admit that she seemed to be equally devoted to him—at first. They married right out of high school. And the trouble didn't start until then, until she came out here to the ranch to live."

"She hated it."

"That's too mild a word. After the first…romantic flush wore off between her and Zach, all she wanted was out of here. She sulked and whined. And she had no pride or sense of privacy. She would start in on him right in the great room, where everyone could hear, or at the dinner table. She would get tears in those big blue eyes and beg him to get her away from here. He would sit there while she complained and pleaded, his face blank, looking like a turtle pulled into its shell, never fighting back more than to cautiously remind her that she had said she wanted what he wanted from life. And, really, it didn't matter what he said. She'd just keep crying and saying she wanted out and she wanted him to go with her."

"But he wouldn't go."

"That's right. And when he wouldn't, she got mean. She threw tantrums. She sulked more than ever. And when she wasn't screaming or sulking or whining, she was criticizing anything and everything. Poor Zach. He didn't know what to do. He still loved her, but she was killing him. His grandfather Ross took him aside and advised that maybe a baby would settle her down. So when she got pregnant, we all had hopes that might make a difference with her. But it didn't. She just got meaner. And in the end, she left and took their baby with her."

Tess got up and refilled their cups.

Edna said, "I honestly thought, for years, that Zach would never take a chance on love again. But then you came along." She reached across the table and patted Tess's hand.

Tess said, "I want to make him happy."

"Oh, you do. I know you do."

As each day went by, Tess felt she understood Zach a little better. Still the emotional chasm between them lay as deep and dangerous as the Grand Canyon.

Tess made no attempt to bridge it. She didn't really know how, though she sensed that complete honesty would be a start.

Complete honesty. Which meant she would have to tell him of those scary feelings she had for him—feelings that each day she became more and more certain added up to love.

And when she told him, how in the world could she expect him to actually believe her? Worse than that, how could she even expect him to care? He'd made it so painfully clear how he felt about love. He wanted nothing to do with it.

Still, he might let her get a little closer to him, if she

could convince him that the specter of Cash no longer stood between them.

Or he might not.

Really, she had no way to know how he would react. And she just wasn't ready to take a chance on finding out.

Not yet, anyway.

On June 16, four weeks and three days after Jobeth broke her arm, the doctor in Buffalo took off the cast.

"I can ride, now. Right?" Jobeth demanded.

"You'll have to be cautious," the doctor warned. "That arm will be weak for a while."

"But can I *ride?*"

"Yes. You may ride."

Jobeth turned to Tess, her eyes as bright as stars. "Mom, I can ride."

"Yes. I heard."

"Let's get home. Right now."

But Edna had ridden with them and both she and Tess had shopping to do. Jobeth managed to contain her impatience until the groceries had been bought.

They arrived back at the ranch at a little before three—and found a dusty but very expensive-looking sports car parked in the turnaround in front of the main house.

"Whose car is that?" Tess asked, thinking Edna might know.

Edna only shrugged. "I haven't the faintest idea. But it appears they've gone on inside, whoever they are. Tim's around here somewhere. He must have let them in."

Tess pulled up in front of the foreman's cottage first. Jobeth leapt from the back seat and headed for the barn almost before Tess got the Suburban to a full stop. Tess considered calling her back and demanding a little help with the groceries, but then she decided to let her go. After all, Jobeth had waited weeks for this moment.

Tess did call out her window, "Don't get on that horse unless Zach or Tim is there to supervise!"

Jobeth turned, grinning widely, running backward in her eagerness. "I won't! I promise!"

"That child," Edna murmured fondly. "Such a dear..."

Tess smiled across the seat at her friend. "Come on. Let's take your things in, then we'll see who our company is."

Tess had gone around to the back of the Suburban and scooped Edna's two shopping bags into her arms when the front door of the main house opened.

A young girl came out—a girl with short, raggedly cut raven black hair. The girl wore a very tight black scrap of a skirt and a black T-shirt cut low enough to show a lot of cleavage and tight enough to reveal every curve of her fully mature torso. She wore no bra under the T-shirt. Stunned at the sight of the girl's lush, unbound breasts beneath the thin layer of cloth, Tess looked down to keep from gawking. The girl wore boots as black as the rest of her outfit—clunky, lace-up boots, with thick soles and round, heavy heels.

Tess straightened, holding a bag in each arm. The girl, looking bored to death, sauntered down the steps and across the yard toward the Suburban. When she got closer, Tess saw that she'd pierced her nose. A diamond caught the sun, winking from the side of her left nostril.

Tess just couldn't help herself. She stared. Even with the bad attitude and the crudely provocative clothes, the girl was drop-dead beautiful. A real traffic-stopper. She had eyes like Elizabeth Taylor's—so blue they appeared violet. Each feature of her face was perfection. And beneath a heavy layer of pale makeup, her skin looked flaw-less.

The girl came within three feet of Tess before she stopped and braced a hand on her hip. The violet eyes gave Tess a long, thorough once-over.

"You must be the new wife," the girl said. "I'm Starr. And I'm here to see my dad."

Chapter Eleven

Tess and Edna exchanged dazed glances. And then Zach rolled into the yard in one of the pickups, with Lolly in the passenger seat and Beau squatting in the truckbed behind the cab. Zach pulled in behind the Suburban.

Hips swaying, Starr strolled to the pickup. As she approached, Beau rose slowly to his feet. He took off his hat and laid it over his heart.

Zach leaned out the window. "Get your tongue back in your mouth, Tisdale."

"Yessir." Beau stuck his hat back on his head and jumped from the pickup bed. "Hi," he said softly to Starr.

Her violet gaze flicked over him dismissively. Her eyes were only for Zach. She stopped right by his door. Cautiously he opened it and climbed down.

Starr smiled at Zach, a smile that taunted—and yet seemed, at the same time, to beg for approval. The diamond in her nose caught the sunlight, glaring. "Hi,

Daddy," she said. "I've had it with Mom. I've decided to come and live with you."

Zach went straight into the house, washed up quickly in the back porch sink and then headed for his office, where he called Leila.

"God, we've been frantic. Frantic." Leila spoke breathlessly. "When did she get there? Is she all right?"

"She just arrived. And she's fine."

"Oh. Of course. *She's* fine. It's the rest of us who are going out of our minds. You would not believe the things she said to me. And to Derek." Derek, Leila's second husband, was rich as Croesus and well into his sixties.

"You had a fight with her?"

"To put it mildly."

"What was the fight about?"

"Everything. You've seen her. The way she dresses. That thing in her nose. How she stays out all night with God knows who and then never bothers to show up at school. And her report card..."

"Bad?"

"Three *D*'s and two *F*'s."

"Damn."

Leila sniffed delicately. "Zach, I don't think I can take it anymore."

Knowing she couldn't see his face, Zach allowed himself an ironic smile. *I don't think I can take it anymore* had been one of Leila's favorite lines, way back when, during the hell that had been their marriage to each other.

Leila had more to say. "I simply cannot handle her anymore. She's totally out of control, *ruining* our lives. She's going to have to repeat her sophomore year. Derek feels we have to draw the line somewhere, and I'm afraid I'm to the point where I agree with him."

"Draw the line. What does that mean, exactly?"

"You don't have to become hostile with me."

"I'm not hostile, Leila."

"Oh, yes you are. I know how you are. Always so calm and logical, while inside, you're just…a seething mass of unresolved anger."

There had been a time when Leila's tongue could really cut into him. But not anymore. Now it just made him feel tired. He said, gently, "Let's talk about Starr, all right? And forget all the old garbage between you and me."

"That was precisely my intention until you started in on me."

"Leila. What do you want to do about our daughter?"

"Well." Leila let out a long breath of air. "You'll just have to keep her, that's all. She'll just have to stay with you for a while."

Zach felt relief then. Even though he knew his daughter would bring trouble, and he had his doubts about his ability to deal with her effectively, he wanted a chance with her. Apparently Leila was willing to let him have that chance. But he had to tread carefully. Leila could be damn vindictive. She had used Starr for years, keeping his daughter away from him as much as possible, just to get back at him. He wouldn't put it past her to change her mind now—if she thought he really *wanted* Starr to stay.

"Zach. Have you hung up?"

"No. I'm still here. And I'm willing to have her stay."

Dead silence, then Leila murmured in an injured tone, "I must say, I'm glad you've decided to be reasonable about this for once."

He refrained from pointing out how often he'd suggested that Starr come and live with him. Leila tended to rewrite the past to suit whatever ax she was grinding at the moment.

"I suppose you'll want me to send some of her things," Leila said.

"Not if they're all skin-tight skirts and combat boots."

"What does that mean?"

"It means I'll make sure she gets the clothes she needs here."

Leila made a small, harsh sound in her throat. "So superior. Always so damn superior."

Zach waited. No way he was going to buy into that one.

Leila said, "I guess, to be fair, I should send back half of this month's support check."

"That's up to you."

"All right. I'll send it back."

"Fine."

"You'll call me. If there's…anything I should know."

"Yeah."

"Well, then. I guess that's all, isn't it?"

He agreed that it was and they said goodbye. When he looked up, he saw Starr lurking in the doorway to the dining room, pulling on a hank of that chopped-off hair. "Well?"

He wanted to order her to wash her face and take that thing out of her nose, but he didn't. He figured demands for changes in her appearance could wait a while. "You can stay."

She dragged in a huge breath and let it out dramatically. "Good. I couldn't go back there, Daddy. I just can't take it with her anymore."

He stared at her, trying to understand why such a good-looking girl would want to wear lipstick the color of dried blood. Watching her, he found himself wondering who the hell she was, anyway. Flesh of his flesh. A total and complete stranger to him. He could see how lost she was.

And not damn likely to be found anytime soon. He thought, How could I have ever let her get this bad off?

"Daddy?" Her smooth black brows drew together over her perfect nose. Even with the punk outfit and all that goo on her face, she was so beautiful, it broke his heart.

"What, Starr?"

"You mad?"

"No."

"You seem mad."

"I'm not." He heard the back door close. It would be Tess, bringing in the groceries he'd seen in the back of the Suburban. A wave of relief swept through him as he thought of his wife and her calm, steady ways. Tess could be counted on. She would help him figure out how to deal with this messed-up almost-woman who also happened to be his child.

"Look," he said. "Tess is bringing in the groceries. Why don't you go on and give her a hand?"

Starr stiffened. "Ex-cuse me? Oh right, I'm going to be treated as a servant or something, is that it?"

Zach stared at her levelly, refusing to be baited. "Go on, Starr. Help Tess."

For a long moment, Starr glared right back at him. Then she shrugged. "Sure, fine. Whatever you say." She turned and left, hips swaying, ridiculous boots clomping.

Zach gave it a good five minutes before he followed his daughter to the kitchen. He found Tess alone, unloading grocery bags. He stood for a moment at the end of the counter, watching her, thinking how soothing just the sight of her could be to a man's troubled mind.

He shouldn't stare at her, and he knew it. The relationship they'd settled on didn't include self-indulgences like staring. But right now, after dealing with Leila and Starr, the sight of Tess was just too comforting to resist.

Tess emptied the bags first, setting their contents on the counter. After that, she folded the bags and set them aside. Then she put what she'd bought in the pantry and the refrigerator, stacking it all neatly, each item in the place she had reserved for it, never wasting movements or space.

"I sent Starr out to help you," he said after he'd watched her so long he could sense her discomfort with his silence. "Did she even come in here?"

Tess picked up a large bag of rice and a few cans of stewed tomatoes. "She was here—and she carried in some bags, too." She turned and disappeared into the pantry, reemerging seconds later, empty-handed. "She said she was going to be staying with us."

"That's right." He realized he probably should have discussed it with Tess before he'd made the final decision. "Is that okay with you?"

"Of course. I sent her out to get her bag from the car."

"Well. That's good."

"She said she didn't bring much."

"Yeah. I just talked to her mother. There wasn't a lot of planning involved in this trip."

Tess lowered her voice. "You mean she got mad at her mother and just took off?"

"Looks that way." He glanced toward the central hall, to make sure his daughter wasn't standing there, listening. "I warned you someday we might have to deal with this."

Tess gave him a calm, direct look. "And I said she would be welcome."

He felt some relief, that she wasn't angry, that she accepted Starr's arrival and all the upheaval it would probably bring. "All right then. I...thank you."

"There's nothing to thank me for. She's your daughter. And she has a place here." Tess leaned back against the rim of the sink and crossed her arms under her breasts. "There's just the one room left upstairs. I already told her to take her things up there."

"Sounds good." He thought of Jobeth then, remembering why Tess had taken her to Buffalo. "Did Jo get her cast off?"

"Yes." Tess tipped her head toward the window over the sink. "She went straight for the barn the minute we got home. She's probably lured that horse with the oat bucket by now. She'll have him tacked up in no time."

"Tim will help her."

"He'd better. I told her not to ride without supervision. She has to watch that arm for a while."

"You know she will. She's a great kid."

"Why is it I have the feeling you're not talking about me?" The voice came from the arch to the central hall. Zach glanced over his shoulder. Sure enough. Starr was there.

Tess explained, "I have a daughter. Her name's Jobeth. She's eight."

"Eight." Starr sneered. "How sweet."

Zach started to tell Starr to watch her mouth. But Tess caught his eye first. She gave a tiny shake of her head. He held his tongue.

Tess said, "Do you ride, Starr?"

Starr stuck out a hip and braced her hand on it. "Yeah. I can ride."

Zach reminded her, "It's been four years since I saw you on a horse."

"They have horses in California, Daddy."

"So you've been riding regularly, is that what you're saying?"

"No, I'm just saying that I have ridden since the last time I was here. I can still ride. If I want to ride."

Tess asked quietly, "*Do* you want to ride?"

Starr looked from Zach to Tess and back to Zach again, as if calculating ahead of time the adult response to her reply. Finally, she answered with a wary question. "Now?"

Tess raised an eyebrow at Zach. "What do you say?"

He shrugged, following Tess's lead, keeping the whole transaction offhand. "Sure. I'll ride with you. We can take Jo, too."

Starr looked pained. "The kid, you mean?"

"She's just learning," Tess warned. "You'd have to take it a little easy with her along."

The violet gaze darted back and forth between the adults, measuring, gauging. Finally Starr forked a black-nailed hand through her spiky hair. "Oh, all right. She can come, I suppose. We'll look out for her."

Tess said, "You'll have to change. Do you have some jeans?"

"Oh, right. Like I'd come to Wyoming without jeans."

Tess smiled. "Then you'd better go put them on."

A half an hour later, Tess watched from the kitchen window as Zach rode past on Ladybird, flanked by Jobeth on Callabash and Starr on a handsome six-year-old mare called Sandygirl.

Edna, who had come over from her own house just a few minutes before to lend a hand with the evening meal, stood beside Tess.

"That girl is so beautiful," Edna said. "I find myself staring at her, marveling at the perfection nature can create. Too bad she has to dress like the bad guy's girlfriend in some awful science fiction movie."

Tess felt the urge to defend Starr. "She did put on jeans, to ride."

"So?"

"Well, the jeans were an improvement on that skirt, don't you think?"

"Not by much. There's still that horrible hair. And all that stuff on her face. And if God had meant for us to poke holes in our noses—"

Tess held up the potato she was peeling as a signal for silence. "Don't say it. You have pierced ears yourself."

"That's different."

Tess just looked at her friend. "Is it?"

Fondly Edna bumped her shoulder against Tess's. "All right. You just may have a point." She lifted an eyebrow at Tess. "But you will try to get her to wear a brassiere, won't you please?"

Tess remembered the dazed, flushed look on Beau Tisdale's face when Starr had strutted down the driveway in his direction. "Definitely. And soon." Tess handed her potato to Edna, who began slicing it thin for au gratin.

"What is it?" Edna asked gently.

Tess realized she'd been staring out the window at nothing. The riders were long gone. She picked up another potato and started in on it with the peeler. "I just think Starr is so sad, that's all. She needs love and attention so much. You can see it in those eyes of hers."

"But she'll reject anyone who tries to offer it," Edna predicted.

"I know."

"You must get together with Zach on this. Really talk this through. Decide what the rules will be for Starr—and then present a united front when she tries to get by you."

"Good advice," Tess said, and wondered, given the careful distance she and Zach maintained with each other, how in the world they would "get together" over the issue of poor, lost Starr.

*   *   *

"I think we should talk. About Starr."

Tess, on the porch step, stared up through the darkness into the shadowed eyes of her husband. "I was thinking the same thing."

His mouth twisted in a wry grin. "I just checked on her. She's up in her room, hooked up by her headphones to that boom box she brought with her. But I've noticed she can be sneaky. I look up and there she is, watching me from a doorway."

"I've noticed that, too."

"Got any carrots in that garden of yours yet?"

She chuckled, feeling so happy that he had sought her out again at last—that he had thought to consult her in this situation with Starr. "My carrots need another good month in the ground. Why?"

"We could wander out to the horse pasture, give them a treat."

"—And, at the same time, be sure no one will hear what we say."

"Exactly."

"How about apples? I bought a bag of them in town today, for pies."

"Get 'em. I'll meet you at the back door."

The horses saw them coming and trotted over, just Ladybird and Callabash at first. But as soon as the others saw the treat, they wandered over, too. Within five minutes, the apple bag was empty.

The horses snorted and nuzzled for more. But when they got nothing but empty hands, they turned one by one and ambled away. Tess folded the empty apple bag and tucked it into a back pocket to put away once she returned to the house.

Zach hoisted himself up to sit on the top rail of the

fence. He looked back toward the house for a moment, then down at Tess. "The last time Starr came here, I told her she had to live by my rules if she wanted to stay with me. That drove her away completely, I think."

Tess could hear the regret in his voice and hastened to point out, "Still, a child does need rules."

"I think so, too. And she remembers, I know she does. She knows that in choosing to come here, she's chosen to do as she's told—at least, to a certain extent. So my bet is that she's going to be on her best behavior for a while."

Tess thought his reasoning made sense. So far, aside from a few snide remarks and sulky looks, Zach's daughter had done everything she'd been told to do. She'd carried in groceries, lugged her bags up to her room and put the sheets on her bed. She'd grudgingly agreed to let "the kid" go riding with her and Zach. She'd even set the table at dinner and helped clear off afterward.

Tess leaned against the fence post. "What do you mean, she'll be on her best behavior *for a while?*"

"I mean, sooner or later she'll be testing us out, trying to push the boundaries."

Tess thought of Starr's sullen looks and snide remarks. "I'm afraid you're probably right."

"So we need clear rules, for when she does start pushing."

"Agreed. Such as?"

"I was thinking a ten o'clock curfew, when she starts chomping at the bit to go out nights. And then only one or two nights a week. She's got to show us we can trust her. And then we'll see about letting her stay out later." He stared back toward the house again. Even in the soft, dim light from the half-moon, Tess could see the worry in his eyes. "I don't know," he said.

"What?"

"Starr. I don't know her at all. Her mother said she's cut a lot of school. Stayed out all night, a lot of nights, with a bad crowd. Her grades were so bad, she'll have to do her sophomore year again. And who knows what else? Drugs?" He met Tess's eyes. She knew he was wondering about the boys Starr might have been staying out all night with—and what exactly she might have been doing with them.

She started to reach out, to put her hand on his knee in a gesture of reassurance. But she stopped herself before she did it. They might be having their first real conversation in days, but that didn't mean he would welcome her touch. She folded her arms over her middle and looked down at the ground, then back up at him. "Let's not borrow trouble, all right? We'll show her she can count on us. Trust us. And we'll show her we expect to be able to trust her. Over time, God willing, she'll open up to us a little."

He made a low noise of agreement. "That's the best we can do, I suppose."

"We'll give her a choice, when it comes to chores. Housework or ranchwork. How's that?"

He groaned. "I hope she chooses the house."

She gave him a look. "Thanks. But she should get a choice."

"All right. And about that thing in her nose…"

"Don't even mention it."

"What?"

"It hurts no one. Not really. And you know it. I'm sure it drove her mother crazy, when she did it. And if it drives us crazy, that's probably enough reason to punch a hole in some other part of her body. Let it be, I'm telling you."

He shook his head. "I hate it, but you're probably

right." His gaze sought hers again. "What about her clothes?"

"She didn't bring much with her. I'll take her shopping."

"I was hoping you'd say that."

"And since this is a ranch, she won't be running around in thigh-high tight skirts too much. I'll try to get her to work with me on choosing appropriate things to wear." Including underwear, she added silently.

He gave a low, humorless laugh. "Somehow, *appropriate* isn't the word that comes to mind when I think about things that Starr might want to wear."

"You'll have to trust me on this," she insisted, with a lot more confidence than she felt.

He was grinning. "Glad to. And good luck."

"Thanks. I'll need it."

They smiled at each other—for just a second too long.

Tess felt the yearning start.

And so did Zach.

His imagination, reined up tight of late, broke free.

He saw himself sliding down from the fence, reaching for her, pulling her close, lowering his mouth to hers the way he had done that night over a week ago on the porch. He remembered the way her body had felt, so soft and pliant, against his. He remembered the sweet, womanly scent of her, the velvet moistness of her mouth when it opened under his.

His own body responded to his thoughts.

He gritted his teeth and reminded himself of how she felt about Cash. For over a week now, all he had to do was focus on that, and any unruly spark of desire would immediately wink out and turn cold.

He ticked off all the things he couldn't afford when it came to her. He couldn't afford to take her to bed. He couldn't afford to let her get too close, or to care about her too much. He couldn't afford to take any emotional risks with her at all, because he'd only end up the loser in the deal. The woman was in love with someone else.

But going over all the things he couldn't afford to do with her didn't help. And the knowledge that she loved his cousin just didn't seem to be working tonight. Tonight, his body didn't give a damn who the hell she loved or how it might hurt in the end if he started loving *her*. He simply wanted her. Wanted to touch and caress. To lose himself in her.

To take away all of her clothes and see her body naked. To kiss all the parts of her that only a husband should kiss. To bury himself in her. To find sweet release.

And then to start all over again...

He had to get the hell away from her, and he had to do it now.

He jumped down from the fence.

She sidestepped neatly, blocking his escape. And she looked at him so tenderly, so hopefully. "Zach..."

He shook his head. "Tess. Let it go."

"Zach, if we could just talk. If I could just explain how I—"

"There's nothing to explain. Just leave it. Please."

"I can't leave it."

"You can. You will."

"This isn't going to work, Zach. Not forever. We can't avoid each other all the time. We can't...feel like this when we finally get a few minutes together and not ever do anything about it. You do...want me, Zach. I can see in your eyes that you do."

"No..."

"Lying won't make the wanting stop."

"I don't—"

"Zach, we are husband and wife. And we have to find our way to each other. Somehow."

"We've been doing fine." He knew as he said the words how stupid and hollow they sounded.

And she knew, too. She looked at him with such sadness in those dark eyes. "Oh, Zach. I understand, at least a little bit, about how bad it must have been, with Leila. I know you're not a man to give your heart easily. And I can see how, the way she hurt you, it's really hard for you to trust a woman again. But I would never hurt you. I swear to you. I'll be true to you until death. I... Oh, Zach. I want you to know something. I have to tell you—"

He put both hands up, as if she held a gun on him, because, dammit, he *felt* as if she did. "Tess. Don't."

"I have to. I have to say it."

"No."

"Yes. I love you, Zach. I do."

Chapter Twelve

Tess stared up at him, hoping, praying, *willing* him to believe her.

But he didn't.

She could see it in his eyes.

He shook his head. "Hell, Tess."

She wanted to grab him, shake him, *make* him believe. "It's true, Zach. I swear it."

He dragged in a long breath and let it out hard. "Look. I think it's time to call it a night."

She wanted to throw herself against him, pound her fists on his chest, *demand* that he give credit to her words. But then she thought of Leila. Leila had made a lot of demands. Zach would only shake his head some more if she acted like Leila.

She drew herself up. "I'm sorry you don't believe me. I can understand why you don't. But I'm glad it's out in the open, anyway. And I sincerely hope that, over time, you will give me a chance to prove the truth of my love for you.''

He looked at her, a sad smile curving his mouth. ''You're a good woman and a good wife. You have nothing to prove to me, Tess. Not a damn thing.''

And with that, he turned and walked away, across the moon-silvered yard to the house. She watched him go, thinking how lonely he looked, longing to run after him—take his hand, walk beside him.

But knowing he would only pull away from her if she tried.

In the days that followed, Tess did her best to keep a positive attitude. She told herself she had done the right thing, that Zach needed to know of her love. And that someday—someday soon—he would come to her and reach out his hand. He would want to know more. He would want her to explain the how and why of her love for him.

And she *would* explain. Everything.

And after that, they would grow closer. Someday—someday soon—they would be husband and wife in every way.

In the meantime, she just had to wait, that was all. Now that her confused feelings for Cash no longer got in the way, she saw all the time how much Zach wanted her, that the looks he gave her when he thought she didn't see would set green wood aflame. He just needed time and space to come to her on his own.

But it was hard not to become discouraged. She wanted to stay positive, but a person had to deal with reality, too.

And reality kept whispering that she'd *been* giving him time and space pretty much since their wedding day. And that it hadn't done a bit of good so far.

* * *

Starr decided she'd rather make beds and scrub pots than work cattle and help with haying. Zach hid a smile of relief when she made her decision. Tess knew he thought that no one noticed. But Tess saw it. She wished they were close. If they had been close, she would have teased him later, when they were alone, about getting off easy in terms of supervising his sulky child.

And Starr *was* sulky. Even in the first few days of her stay at the ranch, she never did anything voluntarily. Direct orders were needed. But at least she did obey orders—reluctantly, wearing a petulant frown.

When Starr had been with them for three days, Tess took her up to Sheridan to buy her some clothes. It turned out to be a relatively painless procedure. Tess chose items she thought appropriate, careful not to suggest anything too frilly or flowery, and Starr said, "Yeah, sure. That's fine. Whatever."

Tess saved the toughest part for last, when she led Starr to the lingerie department. She went straight to the bra racks. "Let's see, Starr. What size are you?"

Starr's lips pulled back from her teeth. "Oh, God. No."

Tess looked up from the rack and into the violet eyes. They stared each other down.

Then Starr said, "I hate them. They bind me up."

"Your breasts are full." Tess kept her tone strictly matter-of-fact. "You need them. At least for riding."

Starr sighed and tossed her head. Her diamond glittered. Then she grunted. "All right. But nothing with wires in it. Please."

The saleslady showed them some brand-new sports bras that gave excellent support without binding. Starr actually smiled when she tried them on. "Hey. These are okay."

After that, Tess didn't have to worry so much about

what the hands might be thinking when Starr walked across the yard.

Four days after the shopping trip, Tess went into the barn through the tack room. She was after some straw to lay between the beds in her garden as a guard against the sun's heat and the moisture loss it caused. She'd just reached the inner door that led to the main part of the barn, when she heard voices.

Jobeth spoke first. "His name is Tick. He's a sweetie, don't you think?"

Then Starr's voice: "Pretty clean, for a barn cat."

"I brush him and Tim gives me stuff to put on his cuts. From the fights he gets in, you know. He's a tom."

Starr laughed. "I know about toms."

"And this is Tack, she's Tick's sister. She's also his wife, I think. Pretty weird, huh?"

Starr agreed, "Yeah. Pretty damn weird."

Jobeth explained, "She'll have kittens, in a few weeks."

A silence.

Tess knew she shouldn't, but she crept sideways, into the shadows, among the bits and bridles strung along the wall. From that angle, she could see the brown head and the black one, bent close together. Each of the girls was busy petting a cat. The cats reveled in the attention, arching their backs, rolling over, nudging and nuzzling at the girls' hands.

The door to the small pasture behind the barn stood open. Bozo stuck his head in. *"Moo-oo-ooo!"* he said hopefully.

"Come on," said Jobeth.

The little steer came in and the girls petted him, too.

Jobeth looked at Starr. "It's hard. Not to care too much about him, you know?"

Starr nodded. She knew as well as Jobeth did that steers were raised to be sold and slaughtered. "Don't let it get you down," Starr said. She reached out and ruffled Jobeth's hair as the steer wandered back out into the sun. "Life's a bust. Then you die. For everybody."

Jobeth grinned. "Life's okay." She looked around the barn. "Especially since we moved here, you know?"

"Yeah, I know. You were like, *born to ranch*. It's all over you."

Jobeth looked at the older girl in frank adoration. "Starr?"

"Yeah?"

"We're sort of sisters, aren't we?"

"Yeah. I suppose."

"Would you mind a lot…if your dad adopted me?"

Starr leaned back against a hay bale and laced her hands behind her head. "Why? Is he?"

"I hope he will."

"Did you ask him?"

"Yeah."

"So what did he say?"

"He said he would talk about it with my mom—when the time's right." Jobeth frowned. "What does that mean, *when the time's right?* Is that one of those things grownups say when they're not going to do anything, really?"

Starr appeared to be playing some kind of ladder game with her fingers.

Jobeth leaned closer. "Whatcha got?"

"Ladybug."

"Cool."

Starr let her hands fall to her lap. They both watched what must have been the ladybug, flying off.

"Fly away home," Jobeth said.

"Yeah, get your ass back to that burnin' house, baby...."

Jobeth let out a guffaw that was part shock and part delight. "Starr!"

"Sorry." Starr leaned against the bale again, sighing—and picked up the conversation about adoption as if it had never been dropped. "No, if my dad says something, he means it. So, he will do it. He'll adopt you. I mean, after he finally gets around to talking to your mom. And *if* your mom says yes."

Jobeth picked up a piece of straw and began smoothing it over her knee. "So would that be okay, with you?"

Starr leaned her head back, closed her eyes.

"Starr. Would it?"

Starr lifted her head again and looked at Jobeth. "Yeah. I wouldn't mind, since it's you. I wouldn't mind at all."

Jobeth said, "Good." For a moment neither girl spoke, then Jobeth declared, "When I get bigger, I'll get a diamond. Just like yours."

"It's only a rhinestone, kid."

"It shines like a diamond. Like you. Like a star."

That night, when Zach came in from his last rounds, Tess was waiting for him in the kitchen.

"What?" he said warily, when he saw her.

She put on a smile that was friendly and no more. "I thought we should touch base a little."

"About what?"

She glanced toward the central hall, to be sure they were alone, and then she lowered her voice. "About Starr."

He frowned. "Did something happen? What did she do?"

Tess stood. "Relax. She didn't do anything. I just want

to talk a little, that's all. Let me get you a beer.'' She waited a fraction of a second, and when he didn't refuse the beer, she went to the refrigerator, pulled out a long-neck and screwed off the top. ''Here.''

He took it, muttering suspiciously, ''Thanks.''

''How about the front porch?''

''Fine.''

He followed her through the house and out the door. She sat in her usual place on the step. He leaned against the porch post opposite her, clearly unwilling to get too close.

He lifted the beer. ''All right. What?'' He drank.

She said, ''The shopping trip went fine.''

He watched her broodingly. ''Yeah, I noticed the jeans and T-shirts. She looks better. Much better.''

Tess knew he also must have noticed that Starr was wearing bras now, but he didn't say anything. He probably thought his troubled daughter's underwear was too intimate a subject to discuss with her. Maybe he thought it would inflame her senses or something, make her grab him and kiss him and say terrible things, like I love you, Zach. And I wish you would give me a chance. I wish you would let me get close, let me tell you everything that's in my foolish heart....

''Anything else?'' he said, already pushing away from the porch post.

No way she was letting him go yet. ''As a matter of fact, yes.''

''I'm listening.''

''I saw her today, in the barn.''

He was instantly on guard. ''With who? Beau?''

''No. With Jobeth.''

He relaxed against the post again.

''What made you think she might be with Beau?''

He drank from his beer. "I don't know. The way he looks at her. And yesterday, I saw them out by the sheds together."

"Doing what?"

He shrugged. "Just talking. It looked like no more than a Hi-how-are-you kind of thing. But it makes me nervous. She's sixteen, with problems. And he's a lonely cowhand. You know what I mean."

She thought of Josh and his green eyes and killer smile, all those years ago. And of her younger self, looking for excitement, for someone to sweep her off her feet. Oh, she did know. She knew exactly what Zach meant.

And yet Starr was so much more sophisticated than Tess had been. What real appeal could some penniless cowpuncher hold for her?

She said, "I've seen the way Beau looks at her. But she didn't seem interested in him in the least. I got the feeling she wouldn't give him the time of day."

"Who can say what goes on with her?"

Tess allowed herself a smug smile. "I can. A little, anyway."

He looked at her sideways. "What does that mean?"

She leaned toward him a little. "I have a theory."

Her enthusiasm must have been contagious. He actually cracked a smile. "A theory, huh?"

"Yes."

"Tell me."

"I believe she really is trying. That she sincerely wants to fit in here, to make things work, with us."

He grunted. "Right. By sulking all the time, making smart-mouth remarks and wearing a ring through her nose."

"It's not a ring. It's a rhinestone."

"Whatever. You know what I mean."

"Zach, aside from you, years ago, I don't think any-body's invested any effort in her at all. I don't think any-body's really cared what she did with herself or her time—until she became an embarrassment, I mean. You should have seen her, when we bought the clothes. Trying to act like she didn't care. But she did care. That someone would take the time to get her outfitted. I swear, I believe her mother probably just threw money at her and told her to get her own clothes."

"But not you," he said softly. "*You* took the time with her."

She looked away. The kind words moved her. Espe-cially coming from him. But she had to be careful not to make too much of them, not to scare him off.

She spoke briskly. "Okay, she doesn't exactly knock herself out to be helpful. But she does what she's told to do. She's keeping the bargain you laid out for her four years ago that if she lives here, she lives by our rules.

"And today, Zach. Today, I went into the barn and saw her with Jobeth. They didn't see me. I probably shouldn't have spied on them, but I did. I hid in the shadows and watched them. And Zach, they are *friends*. I mean, I al-ready noticed that Jobeth thinks Starr is about the most wonderful thing to hit this ranch since Callabash. But Starr cares for her, too. She hides it, when we're around, but you should have seen her, like a real big sister, petting the barn cats and dishing out advice about how tough life can be. And then...grabbing Jobeth, ruffling her hair. Jo-beth said that they were like sisters, weren't they? And Starr nodded and said she supposed that they were."

Tess glanced away for a moment, remembering the other subject the girls had discussed—the subject of Zach adopting Jobeth. Tess had stewed about that all afternoon. And then she'd accepted the fact that for Jobeth to be

Zach's child legally could only be for the best, no matter what happened in the end between herself and Zach.

If Jobeth were legally Zach's daughter, then she would never lose her place with him, or on this ranch. It would break Tess's heart in two, to have to let her daughter go, should it come to that. But she would do it. If that was Jobeth's choice, and if Zach wanted it, too.

Still, Tess had no intention of mentioning the adoption issue herself. It was Zach's subject to broach.

Zach tapped his empty beer bottle against his thigh. "Well. What you've told me sounds...interesting."

"Come on," she scoffed. "You know it's much more than *interesting*. It's progress, that's what it is." She considered telling him a bit more—such as how Jobeth admired Starr so much, she planned to get her nose pierced. But then she decided that probably wouldn't go over real big.

"What else?" he demanded.

"Nothing."

"I can see by that smile that there's something else."

"No," she said, playing innocent. "Not a thing. That was it."

He leaned his head back against the post and let out a breath. "Well. I guess you're right. It does sound like maybe Starr is working to get along, like maybe she *wants* to be here. And that's good."

"Yes. Very good."

A silence fell. The night sounds, imperceptible a moment ago, seemed much louder. Tess heard the soft whicker of one of the horses out in the back pasture, carried to them on the wind. And some bird she couldn't identify trilled out a long, sweet cry somewhere off to the east. And far off, as always, the coyotes howled.

Zach said, "Well..." He pushed himself away from the

post and started for the door. He was leaving her, as he always left her, sitting in the darkness, alone.

"Zach."

He turned, his hand on the doorknob. "Yeah?"

"I've been wondering."

His eyes narrowed. "What?"

She cast about for something—anything—to keep him there a few moments longer.

"What is it, Tess?" Impatient. Eager to get away.

A subject finally occurred to her. "Well...about the rustling problem."

"What about it?"

"You haven't mentioned anything lately, about signs of trouble out in the pastures."

"Nobody's seen anything—not since Beau and Tim found those tire tracks back at the end of May."

"Almost a month ago," she said. "That's good, isn't it?"

He shrugged. "Could be. Who can say?"

"Maybe they've stopped."

"It's possible."

"But you don't think so."

"No, I don't. I think they've been smart and lucky. And that we've never been at the right place at the right time.

"And I think anytime you ride out by yourself, you should be sure and take that little Colt I gave you."

Chapter Thirteen

"It's hot," Jobeth whined.

"It's unbearable," Starr agreed. She was sitting next to Jobeth, on the top step of the front porch. She leaned her head against the porch post and groaned aloud. "What we need is a swim."

Tess and Edna, who sat back in the shadows of the porch, hemming twin panels of a set of curtains Tess had made for Starr's room, shared a smile at the girls' complaining.

Edna rubbed sweat from the bridge of her nose, sliding thumb and forefinger under the glasses she wore for close work. "Oh, yes. It feels like August and it's hardly the end of June."

"Mom," Jobeth said.

"Um?"

"When are Zach and the others coming back?" They

had headed out after the big noon meal, to fix a length of fence near the highway into town.

"I don't know," Tess said. "Anytime now, I'd guess."

"We could ride out to meet them." Jobeth looked at her stepsister with hopeful eyes.

Starr made a grotesque face, sticking out her tongue and rolling her lips back away from her teeth. "*Ugh*. Just what I need on a scorcher like this. To get on the back of some sweaty, fly-bitten nag and ride along a dusty road to meet up with my dad and two cowboys."

"Sandygirl's no nag."

"She's a horse. Horses sweat. They draw flies. I am not getting on a horse unless I'm riding it someplace I can swim. Get it?"

"Yeah. I get it." Jobeth gave Starr a nudge with the toe of her tennis shoe. "Meany."

Starr nudged back, playfully, with a bare foot.

"Hey!" Jobeth gave Starr a shove.

"Watch it...." Starr shoved back.

Seconds later, they were rolling around together on the little patch of scrubby grass at the foot of the steps, squealing and giggling. Tess and Edna shared another look and went on with their sewing.

Right then, Zach and the men drove into the yard. With a sigh, Tess stood from her comfortable swing chair. She gave a long whistle. The girls froze and looked up at her.

She pointed at the pickup. The girls pulled apart and jumped to their feet. Zach drove past them, no doubt on the way to park in the tractor barn on the far side of the sheds out in back. He waved as he went by—and so did Beau, who rode in the truckbed with the tools, the barb-wire, and the leftover posts.

Tess glanced immediately at Starr, to see how she re-acted to the sight of Beau. The girl appeared more interested in yanking her cutoffs back into place after her wrestling match with Jobeth than in making eyes at the ranch hand. Starr looked up and caught Tess's glance. "Listen, Tess. Crystal Creek runs along on the other side of the horse pasture, behind that old cabin where Great-grandpa John used to live. We can ride above the bank until we find a decent place to swim. Let me take Jo and go. We'll be back by five, I swear."

Tess had been wary of letting either of the girls head out for isolated spots. If those cattle thieves were still doing their dirty work on the Rising Sun, she didn't want Jobeth or Starr meeting up with them.

"Tess. *Please*. We are suffering here."

Tess chewed on her lower lip a little, thinking she wouldn't mind a swim herself, but she did need to get started on dinner soon.

Edna said, "You take them. I'll get the dinner going."

Tess grinned. "Mind reader. I owe you one."

"Good. Scrabble. This evening at my house. You'll let me win and pretend you didn't."

"We can go?" Starr asked, looking hopeful and younger than her years for once.

"Yes," Tess said. "Let's get our suits on and saddle up."

They'd caught the horses and were cinching up saddles when Zach came out of the barn and strode their way. Tess looked up and saw him coming. Patches of sweat darkened his old blue shirt, down the front and under the arms. Lines of sweaty dust had collected in the creases of his neck. His jeans were gray with dirt. Tess thought she'd never in her life seen a better-looking man.

He asked, "What's up?"

Tess told her silly heart to settle down and answered

with a calm she wished she could feel in his presence, "We're going hunting. For a swimming hole."

His glance flicked to the Colt at her hip. "You'll be careful."

"You know we will."

The little gray mare she'd chosen whickered softly. Tess patted her forehead. "Easy. It's okay."

The girls were already mounted and ready to go. Reggie, who'd appeared from the barn when they started tacking up, sat to the side, waiting patiently, looking expectant. Tess swung into the saddle. As she fiddled with the reins, Zach stepped up and took the headstall. She looked down at him. He smiled. She felt weakness all through herself. Longing that could hardly be borne. Yet she would bear it.

He gave her a crooked smile. "I'll get a shovel and follow along. If you don't find a good hole, we can make one."

She watched his mouth, wishing she could just bend down and plant a kiss on it.

He asked, "So what do you say?"

"Sounds good."

He started giving instructions. "Okay then, pick up the creek down behind the old cabin. Follow it about two or three miles, toward the mountains. You'll be on public land that nobody's been using this season. You should find some good places there." Tess took his meaning. Cattle tended to break down the banks of streams and flatten out the streambeds. On unused land, the creek would be more likely to keep a deeper channel. "I'll be along, in a few minutes." He let go of the bridle and backed away.

The girls started off and Tess followed after them, Reggie taking up the rear.

* * *

A half an hour later, they found a good spot, a wide bend in the creek that slowed down the water. It wasn't that deep. But it was clear and inviting. Cottonwoods and willows grew close to the bank, providing tempting, welcome shade.

Reggie flopped down in the shade as the girls quickly dismounted and stripped off their clothes, revealing the bathing suits they'd put on underneath. They ran for the bank, hooting like wild animals, yowling in glee when they hit the water, going under for several seconds and then shooting up in the air, shivering and screaming.

"It's cold!"

"It's *freezing!*"

"It's great!"

Tess spread an old blanket in the shade of a cottonwood and removed her own jeans, shirt and boots at a more sedate pace. She felt nervous, knowing Zach would come. She hoped she looked all right in her three-year-old suit. In the bright sun, the tropical print seemed just a little faded, she thought. Still, the colors were pretty and complemented her skin tone. And the cut was modest, so she didn't feel *too* naked.

"Tess, come on! Hurry up!"

"Yeah, Mom! Get in!"

She adjusted the straps of her suit, then turned toward the clear water and the waving, shouting girls. "Look out! I'm coming!" She took off at a run, pausing a split second at the edge to jump and gather her legs up to her chest. Shrieking, she sailed out across the creek, hitting the surface in a beauty of a cannonball, sending water flying everywhere.

Zach heard all the screeching and shouting a quarter of a mile away. He slowed Ladybird and listened. The sounds told him that Tess and the girls had found a perfectly fine place to swim and wouldn't need him or his shovel after all. He might as well turn back.

But he didn't turn back. He just kept on moving toward the laughter and happy voices. Finally he came up a small rise and there they were below him, not thirty feet away. He reined in. Leaning on the saddle horn, he watched one doozy of a water fight—a battle in which Starr showed herself willing to play dirty, but Tess definitely had the best hand for serious water spraying. Jobeth, outsized and outclassed, mostly cowered between the other two, squealing and howling.

Tess, as pretty as a mermaid in a suit with big, bright flowers all over it, spotted him first. She stopped and tried to wave, which gave Starr a chance to mount a serious attack.

"Come on, Jo!" Starr commanded, fanning water hard and fast at a disadvantaged Tess. "Get her! Help me get her!"

Jobeth turned on her mother with glee. The two girls sprayed and splashed until Tess dived beneath the surface. The girls looked around. Tess came up near the bank and started right for the edge.

"No fair! Chicken!"

Tess waved a hand at them, hardly glancing back, leaving them to turn on each other—which they immediately did.

"Zach. You came." Her slanted eyes were on him, only on him, as his eyes were only for her. Right then, their splashing, giggling daughters might not have existed.

She emerged from the creek, her long, slim legs revealed to him for what must have been the first time. She looked so good, the water running off of her—she looked *womanly*, everything sleek and strong and yet soft at the same time.

When she got up on the bank, she kept coming toward him. He watched her come, knowing she felt his gaze on her, though his eyes were shadowed by the brim of his hat. At a blanket spread beneath a cottonwood, near where Reggie lay asleep, she stopped to scoop up a towel, then came the rest of the way, drying herself as she walked.

I love you, she had told him the other night.

He didn't believe it. He knew it couldn't be true.

But damn. It had sounded good.

And now, looking into her welcoming eyes as she came on, he didn't know if he even cared anymore who she loved or how she might hurt him if he let himself get too attached to her.

He was already attached to her.

He couldn't imagine his life without her.

He might as well go ahead and surrender all the way to her.

Because she was going to have him in the end.

As he would have her.

Sitting there on his horse as his wife approached him on that hot June day, Zach Bravo at last came to understand that it was only a matter of time. He would keep her at bay as long as he could bear to—keep his pride and his distance till he just plain couldn't stand not having her. But sooner or later, he would fall.

She stopped a few feet from him and rubbed her hair with the towel. He watched the tender flesh of her inner arm, the hollow where her arm met her body, the slight rounding of her breast before it disappeared under the suit. She went on rubbing, drying her hair. His gaze trailed up, over the sweet curve of her shoulder and the singing line of her neck. He met her eyes and saw a woman's knowledge.

She knew exactly what she was doing, drying her hair that way, looking at him so steadily, a half smile on that mouth of hers.

Maybe he didn't have her love. But he had her desire. She wanted him now—as she had not on their wedding night. Now, when he took her, he would be able to tell himself it was his own face she saw when she closed her eyes.

That was something.

Not enough for him, but better than nothing at all.

"Come swimming," she said, hooking the towel around her neck.

"Naw." He reached back to put his hand on the shovel he'd tied behind his saddle. "I just came in case you needed help."

She gestured over her shoulder. "We found the perfect spot. And the water's great."

Starr yelled and waved from the bank across the stream. "Daddy! Come on!"

Jobeth, standing beside Starr, chimed in. "Yeah, Zach, come swim!"

He shook his head and waved. "Some other time!"

The two girls groaned in unison, then jumped back in the water and started splashing each other again. Watching them, Zach thought that Starr really did seem to be coming out of her sulky shell more and more every day. He also remembered the promise he'd made to Jobeth a while back. He would have to talk to Tess about it soon.

He saw no reason that she would say no. His adopting Jobeth would only give his stepdaughter a firmer claim on the land she loved so much. Still, he hesitated to bring the subject up with Tess. Somewhere inside himself, he couldn't help fearing that she would turn his offer down. Maybe it was all the years of dealing with Leila. It had ruined him for thinking a woman would ever do the right thing when it came to her own child.

"Thanks for coming to help." Tess stepped forward and took Ladybird's bridle the way he had done with her gray mare back at the horse pasture. "—Even if we didn't need you in the end." She patted the horse's neck and smiled up at him.

Something softened deep inside him. She was not like Leila. Not in any way. She would be kind in her power over him.

And she *was* fair.

He said quietly, "Jobeth would like me to adopt her."

She went on smiling, though the smile changed, grew tender and a little bit sad. "I know."

"Will you allow that?"

"Yes, Zach. I will."

Zach and Tess drove to Buffalo the next day to consult with the family lawyer, Philo T. O'Hare. O'Hare said that since Jobeth's natural father was deceased and Tess was the girl's sole guardian, the adoption should be no problem at all. He had them fill out a petition for adoption and assured them that the finalizing court date would occur within a month or so.

Tess seemed lost in her own thoughts on the way back. Zach didn't disturb her. He felt good, to know that within weeks, he could claim Jobeth as a true daughter. He also felt grateful to his wife, for granting him that claim.

At home, the girls and Edna were waiting for them, hungry for news of how it had gone.

"You'll be a Bravo within a month or two," Zach told Jobeth.

She let out a yelp of glee and launched herself at him, hugging him hard. From him, she jumped on Starr, then she grabbed Edna and squeezed her a good one.

Last of all, she went into her mother's waiting arms.

"Oh, thanks, Mom," she said. "Thank you so much."

"There's nothing to thank me for," Tess replied. "It's the best thing. The right thing."

"Oh, Mom. It is. I know it is."

They rang the bell for the hands and then went in to the midday meal that Edna had prepared.

After they ate, Zach decided to take Jobeth out to poison weeds. He invited Starr. She grunted. "No, thanks. I think I'll stick around here."

"You still have vacuuming to do, young lady," Edna reminded her.

"I know, I know. It's just a thrill a minute around this place." The words were sarcastic, but then she grinned.

Zach congratulated himself again on how much progress they were making with her.

An hour later, in her swinging chair on the front porch, Tess tied off the last stitch on the last hem of the last panel of Starr's new midnight blue curtains. By then, Zach and Jobeth were long gone, and Edna had wandered back across the yard to her own house for a brief nap. Starr was inside—presumably dusting, but probably sprawled across her bed with her headphones on, thumbing through one of her rock and roll magazines.

Humming happily to herself, Tess rose and carried the final two panels she'd been working on inside. The other four panels were folded and waiting in the master bedroom. Tess had set up her sewing machine in there, as well as the iron, all hot and ready for a final pressing. Tess ran the iron over the curtains.

Then she carried her handiwork across the hall to Starr's room. At the door, she gave a light knock. "Starr?"

No answer. The girl probably had her headphones cranked up loud. Tess peeked around the door. No Starr. Tess shrugged. Who could ever say where that girl might get off to? She was probably out in the barn, leaning against a hay bale, woolgathering.

Tess went on into the room, set the curtains on the midnight blue quilted spread she'd made a few days before and returned to her own room for the stepladder she kept in the closet there. Back in Starr's room, Tess set up the ladder, grabbed a curtain rod and began feeding a panel onto the end. Once she had the curtains strung on the rods, she moved to the window to hook the rods in place.

She'd just raised her foot to the first step of the footstool when she looked down on the backyard—and caught sight of Beau Tisdale as he pulled a very willing-looking Starr through the open door of the barn.

Chapter Fourteen

For an endless moment, Tess just stood there with one foot on the stepladder, staring blindly out the window at the door of the barn, wishing with all of her heart that she hadn't seen what she'd just seen.

Already, the cowhand and Zach's daughter had disappeared into the shadows beyond the door. Nothing marked their passing. If Tess had looked down a few seconds later, she wouldn't even have seen them.

And some part of her truly wished that she hadn't. Because some part of her—a very large part of her—did not want to deal with this at all.

Carefully Tess carried the curtains and rods back to the bed and set the whole apparatus down. Then, for several minutes, she just stood there, looking at her own handiwork, trying to decide what action she should take here.

Starr was sixteen. And probably not a complete innocent.

Beau had to be at least in his twenties. At this point in their lives, he was too old for Starr. Wasn't he? The law would certainly say so.

Tess put her hands to her mouth, shook her head.

And thought of Josh.

And the act she had done with him that had changed her life so irrevocably. The act that had created Jobeth, who was more precious to Tess than her own life.

No, Tess would never choose *not* to have had Jobeth, no matter what the price.

But, Jobeth aside—oh, to go back! To simply not make that choice to lie down in the barn with her father's hired man. To have been valedictorian of her high school class, as she would have been. To have gone off on an AG scholarship to college. To have been there when her father died, and to have done all she could to keep her place, her home, her heritage.

All those possibilities wiped out.

Because of a handsome man and an urge to wildness inside herself.

If, somehow, her parents had found out before it was too late—if they had talked to her—would it have changed anything?

Tess couldn't be sure. She just wasn't that girl anymore, that girl who flung herself at life without a care for the cost. That girl who was a lot like Starr—not so tough or so worldly-wise, maybe. But bright and passionate and hungry to see what the world had to offer.

Tess found she was turning for the stairs.

Maybe it would do no good. Maybe she had no right to intervene. Maybe she should wait for Zach to come home and discuss the situation with him, call him on that cellular phone he carried in the pickup with him now and tell him to hurry home.

But he couldn't get home fast enough to keep whatever was going on out in the barn from proceeding right through to its natural conclusion.

Which might be totally innocent.

Or might not...

No, she couldn't let it go. Not even for the time it would take Zach to come home and deal with it. She had to do what she could right now.

Tess went down the stairs, through the kitchen and out the back door, closing it rather loudly behind her, making no secret of her whereabouts. She marched straight for the barn and went right inside.

At first glance, it appeared deserted. And then she heard the rustling behind a stack of hay bales in the corner.

"Starr."

More rustling.

"Come on out. Now."

Slowly, her faced flushed and hay in her hair, Starr emerged from behind the bales. Tess stared at her, not sure what to do next. Starr stared right back, defiant.

Finally Tess managed to speak in a dry whisper. "You buttoned your shirt crooked."

Starr's lower lip quivered as she swiftly corrected the problem.

"Beau," Tess said more strongly. "Are you just going to hide back there and let Starr face the music alone?"

Beau appeared behind Starr, looking grim. All of his clothes seemed buttoned up right. Tess dared to hope that was because he'd never *un*buttoned anything. He had his hat in his hand and he beat it a few times against his thigh, watching Tess warily as he did it.

"You'd better go on back to your trailer for now," Tess told him.

His jaw twitched. For a moment, Tess thought he might argue with her. But then he turned without a word and started toward the door, brushing bits of hay from his shirt and hair as he went.

Starr watched him go, a look of injured disbelief on her beautiful face. She let him get all the way to the door, before she called out, "Beau! Wait! You don't have to do what *she* says. You don't have to..." She let the sentence die unfinished when Beau only shook his head and kept on walking.

Fuming now, Starr turned back to Tess. "Nice going. Thanks."

Tess stared at her stepdaughter. "The attitude won't work on me, Starr."

"What the hell are you talking about?"

"Attacking me isn't going to make this situation disappear—or keep me from telling your father about it."

Starr let out a disgusted breath, braced a hand on her hip and looked Tess up and down. "And I thought you were all right."

Tess only sighed. "I can see we're not going to get anywhere right now. Just go on up to your room. I'll send your father up after he gets home."

Starr was chewing on her lower lip. For a moment, Tess thought she might break down, say something honest, open the door for a real talk.

But in the end, she only drew back her shoulders and lifted her perfect chin. "Fine." Her rhinestone glinted; her eyes flashed in pure scorn. "And anyway, I know what's up with you. I know why you're making such a big deal out of this."

Dread formed, a hard ball, in Tess's stomach. "Starr, look—"

"I *am* sixteen. I've got a brain. And eyes. I know you

and my dad aren't married in any *normal* way. Because I know where my dad sleeps. And it's not with you.''

Tess felt as if the girl had kneed her in the stomach. But somehow, she stayed upright and continued looking Starr right in the eye. ''My relationship with your father has nothing to do with this. And I think you know that.''

Another stare-down ensued. In the end, Starr's bravado cracked. She let out a tiny cry, whirled on her heel and ran from the barn.

Tess watched her through the wide-open door, made sure she ran toward the house and then listened for the slam of the back door. When she heard it, she found a hay bale and carefully lowered herself onto it. She sat there for a long time, staring at the rough floor, feeling numb and awful. She had thought that everything was going so well lately.

So much for what she had thought.

Zach and Jobeth stood out in a pasture near Saunderman Road, staring down at the tire tracks and the dragged spot the stock trailer ramp would have made.

''Is it them, Zach? Were the rustlers here?''

''Looks like it. Get me the phone from the pickup, will you?''

Jobeth took off. She was back with the phone in a flash. ''Here you go.''

Zach punched up the auto-dial number for the sheriff's office in Buffalo, got the dispatcher and explained what he'd seen, where he was and how to get there. Then he handed the phone back to Jobeth, who trotted to the pickup, put it away and ran back to him once more.

''What do we do now, Zach?''

''We wait for someone to come out and write a report.''

* * *

Zach and Jobeth arrived home at five-thirty, both covered in mud. They left their boots by the back door and came trooping in in stocking feet.

Tess knew from the look on Zach's face that the afternoon had been no better for him than for her. "What happened?"

"We found tire tracks," Jobeth said eagerly. "Ones the rustlers must have left. So we called the range detective and he came out to make a report." From over at the stove, Edna made a sound of distress. Jobeth continued, "We got all this mud on us later, from pushing the pickup out of a mudhole."

Tess looked at Zach. "Do you know how many cattle are missing?"

"No way to be sure," he said flatly, "as usual." His tone grew brisk. "We need to clean up. Come on, Jo." The two headed upstairs to their respective showers.

Tess trailed after them to the foot of the stairs, dismayed at the news about the tire tracks, and worried about Starr, all alone in her room, probably fretting and fuming, wondering when her father would come. The girl had been up there for almost three hours now. It was long enough for her to suffer and wonder. And really, Tess thought, someone ought to go out and talk to Beau, too. Probably Zach. But Zach couldn't talk to anybody if he didn't know what was going on. And Tess didn't see how she would get Zach alone to share a word with him for hours yet. Sighing, she wandered back into the kitchen, wiping her hands on her apron, trying to remember what had to be done next to get the dinner on the table and everyone fed.

Edna, still at the stove stirring the beans, tapped the spoon impatiently against the rim of the pot. "Tess, you are nervous as a sinner in church. Something isn't right—

beyond the news about those thieves. And where is Starr, anyway? We could use a little help with the table.''

Tess hadn't planned to mention anything to Edna about the incident in the barn, at least not until she'd spoken with Zach—but then she turned and met her friend's eyes.

Edna set the spoon on the spoon rest. ''All right. What's happened with Starr?''

Tess shot a glance around to be sure that they were alone. Then she swiftly explained the events of the afternoon—minus only Starr's comment about where she and Zach slept at night.

Edna said, ''You must talk to your husband immediately.''

''I know. But there's no time now.''

''Of course there is. You just run on upstairs and catch him before he comes down from his shower.''

Tess gaped at her friend. ''Run upstairs? Now?''

''Yes.''

Tess knew Edna's suggestion made perfect sense. She should have just followed Zach upstairs to his room in the first place and caught him alone. And yet she hadn't. Because she *never* entered his private space—except to gather his laundry when she washed his clothes. He made his own bed and tidied up after himself. With the kind of relationship they had, she wouldn't dare go near him when he was in his room. And never *ever* when he was doing something so private as taking a shower.

''Tess. What is the matter with you?''

''Nothing. Really. It's just that I'm so worried. About Starr.''

''Well, then. Go talk it over with Zach. Now.''

''But the dinner—''

''Oh, come on. I've been getting dinners on the table in this house for more years than I care to count. I think

I can manage it this evening. I'll feed the hands and Jobeth and myself. You worry about Zach and Starr.''

"Yes. You're right. I know you are."

"So get going."

"Yes. I am. Right now."

Tess stood in the upstairs hall, her ear pressed against Zach's door. The shower stopped. She would give it a slow count of two hundred, and then she'd knock.

"Mom?"

Tess let out a cry and turned. Jobeth stood at the top of the stairs, her hair slicked back and her skin still rosy from her own shower.

"Mom, what are you doing?"

"Jobeth, you scared me."

"Sorry. But what are you—?"

"Honey, I need to talk to Zach."

"Oh."

"Go on down and help Edna with the dinner."

"Okay. Where's Starr?"

"In her room."

"Can I get her?"

"Uh, no. We'll bring her. When we come."

"But—"

"Jobeth, would you please just do what I asked you to do?"

Frowning, Jobeth studied her mother. "Something's strange. What's wrong with you?"

"Nothing's wrong with me." That wasn't a lie, not exactly. "I promise you. I am fine. Now please go on down and give Edna a hand."

Reluctantly Jobeth descended the stairs. Tess moved to the top of the stairwell and watched her go, willing her not to change her mind and decide to come back up.

Finally Jobeth reached the bottom step and disappeared in the direction of the kitchen. Tess heard Edna's voice, faintly. "There you are. Come and set the table, please."

Good, Tess thought. Edna would keep Jobeth out of the way now. Tess turned for Zach's door once more.

It was open. Zach stood in the doorway, wearing clean Wranglers—and nothing else.

Tess blinked and stammered. "Oh. I didn't—"

"What the hell's going on?"

"I…" She gulped and stared and felt like a complete fool. "I have to talk with you."

"Right now?"

"Yes. And in private. Please."

He gave her one of those long looks of his, a look that measured and doubted and made her feel so confused. Then he stepped back. "All right. Come on."

She moved past him into the room, far too aware of his strong, bare chest, of the steam in the air, left over from his shower, of the clean scent of soap that came from his skin. He closed the door behind her, closed them in together…

She headed for the chair in the corner—as far away from him as she could get, thinking, Come on, get a grip here. This is about Starr, not about all the things you wish your husband would do to you that he *won't* do to you. She sat, drew her shoulders back, sucked in a good, long breath.

Zach remained by the door, watching. "Talk."

Suddenly she couldn't bear to sit. She stood. She went to the window and looked out at the barn, at the door through which Beau had pulled Starr only a few hours before.

The way to explain it all finally came to her. She would

just start with herself at the window in the room next door and go right on through till the end.

So she did. She told it all, everything, right up to when Edna had sent her upstairs to talk to him. Everything *except* Starr's remarks about their sleeping arrangements. Somehow, she just couldn't admit that part. And really, it wasn't the issue anyway.

By the time she'd finished, Zach was already turning to the bureau, pulling out a white T-shirt and clean socks. She added, "I honestly thought it was going so well with her. I just…I had no idea about this thing with Beau."

Zach tugged the shirt over his head. "I told you I was suspicious. But we couldn't be sure anything was going on until now. Did you talk to her at all? Did you get any sense of how far the two of them have carried this?"

"No. She was so hostile. I just…didn't know how to reach her."

"It's all right," he said. "You did what you could. " He sat briefly and put on the socks. Then he went to the closet and got some boots. He sat a second time, just long enough to yank them on. Finally he stood.

Tess met his eyes. "I thought it might be good, to let her think things over for a while. But maybe I took it too far. She's been in there for hours, waiting. I believe I heard her go into the bathroom once, but that's all. I kept thinking you and Jobeth would show up, so I just left her in there. I probably should have—"

He waved a hand. "You did fine. I'll go talk to her now."

"And to Beau."

"He'll be next. Starr first."

"Yes. Good."

He turned and went out. Tess sank back to the chair, unwilling to go downstairs until he came out of Starr's room, just in case—well, she wasn't sure what. She only knew she wanted to be there waiting when Zach came out. So she stayed.

Zach tapped on Starr's door.

A moment, later, she pulled it open partway and peered out at him. "What?" Her eyes were hard and cold.

"Let me in."

Starr flung back the door and faced him. Behind her, he could see her bed, littered with magazines, her discarded headphones tossed on top of the heap. Over in the corner, wadded up in a pile, lay what looked like the dark blue curtains Tess had been making for her. The stepladder stood a few feet from the wad of blue cloth.

Starr saw the direction of his gaze. She made a low, guilty sound in her throat. "Look. Those stupid curtains were in my way. All right?"

He crossed the threshold and closed the door behind him. For a moment, the two of them stared at each other. Zach had a feeling of total unreality. He didn't know what to do. Or how to begin.

Starr threw up her hands. "Okay. Say it. I have to go, right? You don't want me around anymore because I'm just...too trampy to live here. Right? Because I have to live by your rules and I blew your rules, going back behind the hay bales with Beau."

He focused on what he was sure of. "Starr. I don't want you to leave."

She dropped to the edge of her bed, to the one spot not littered with magazines. "You don't?" Her eyes seemed to ask, So what's the catch?

Zach despised himself then. How in the hell had he let her get so far away from him that she didn't believe she could get back? "You live here. With us."

The pile of magazines started to slide in her direction. She shoved at it with her elbow. "*She* hates me now."

"Tess does not hate you. She's worried about you."

"She'll tell Jo to keep away from me."

"No, she won't."

Starr looked down at all the magazines, then out toward the window.

"Starr. Look at me."

Her head snapped around and she glared at him, her mouth set in a mutinous line. "I'm not a tramp. I'm not."

"No one called you a tramp."

"*They* did. Derek and Mother. They called me worse than that. But I'm not. I don't do drugs. And I don't do anything with guys. I know how guys are. I learned early. When it comes to guys, it's simple. If you don't get humped, you don't get dumped."

Zach cleared his throat. "That's an...interesting way of putting it."

"It's the truth, that's all." She sniffed and wiped her nose with the back of her hand. "But Beau, he's different than other guys." Personally Zach thought Beau was a weasel and a snake in the grass. But he kept his opinion to himself.

Starr must have seen something in Zach's expression that betrayed his opinion of Beau. She cried, "I can tell you blame him!"

"Starr. What he did was wrong."

"But he *cares* for me. He does."

"Then why didn't he come knocking on the front door and ask for you?"

She glared. "And what would you have said if he did?"

"I would have said no."

"Exactly. So I had to sneak out to see him. I'm not proud of it, but what else could we do?"

Zach thought, Stayed away from each other. But he didn't say it. It would have done no good.

Starr had more to say. "Oh, Daddy, Beau *is* different than other guys. He understands what it's like to have everyone making judgments on you, deciding you're a certain way. Because of how you dress. Or because of what your family is like. He hasn't had an easy life, you know. He lost everything. And his father's always drunk now, since they lost their ranch. And his brothers get in trouble all the time. That's not easy for a man to live with, you know?"

"It seems like you've learned a lot about him."

Starr studied her thumbnail, which was coated with a thick layer of purple polish.

"Starr, you said you'd been sneaking out to see him."

She began chewing on her cuticle. "He cares about me. He really does."

"Starr."

She pressed her lips together, recrossed her legs, shoved at the magazine pile again.

Zach tried to think of a way to reach her. He imagined what Tess might do. It came to him that Tess would get closer to her.

He moved toward Starr. She stopped chewing on her cuticle and watched him suspiciously. When he stood right before her, he dropped to a crouch, so he was the one looking up. "Starr. How many times have you sneaked out at night to…talk with Beau?"

She just stared at him. He waited. Finally she admitted in a small, lost voice, "I don't know. Six or seven."

He swallowed and sucked in a breath. "Look. I'm not judging you. I don't have the right. I haven't been…around enough to go judging you. But I have to know, if the two of you have…" He coughed. He was a reserved man. A *conservative* man. "I hate asking this."

The tears were there, now, in those beautiful blue eyes. "We haven't, Daddy. I swear. I…do care for him. And I probably *would* have. Soon. But not yet. Honest." She looked at him long and hard, as though *willing* him to believe her. Then, with a sad little hitch of her breath, she hung her head and swiped her nose with the back of her hand again.

He dared to reach out, to smooth her spiky hair. "It's okay. It'll be okay."

She only shook her head and kept looking down toward her bare toes that were painted the same intense purple as her fingernails. Outside, someone started banging on the dinner bell. Zach rose.

Starr looked up at him then, desperation in her eyes. "Don't fire him. I'll keep away from him. He needs this job, Daddy."

"What he's done is wrong. He's a grown man. And you're under eighteen. I can't trust a man like that. You have to see that."

"No. Please. You said you wouldn't judge me. Well, don't judge him, either. Give him a chance. Talk to him. You'll see. He does care for me."

"That's not the point."

"Just talk to him first. Please."

He studied her face, not knowing what to say to her. *"Please?"*

He couldn't completely refuse her. "All right. I'll talk to him first. But I really can't see how anything he could say would make me willing to keep him on."

"Just give him a chance."

"Starr—"

"All right, all right. As long as you listen to what he tells you. As long as you do that much."

"I said that I would. Now, why don't you go on down to dinner?"

"No. I'll just stay here. I couldn't eat. Not tonight."

He didn't argue with her. "We'll talk more later."

"Yeah. Okay."

Tess heard Zach come out of Starr's room. He went on down the stairs. She rose from the chair in the corner and almost followed him. But to what purpose? If he wanted to talk to her, Edna would tell him she was still upstairs. And if he just aimed to deal with Beau and get it over with, she didn't want to slow him down.

She sank back to the chair. She knew she probably ought to go ahead and join the others at the table. But she just wasn't quite up to that prospect right then. No, she'd just sit here for a bit, in the quiet room that had so much of Zach in it. She'd take some deep breaths and say a little prayer or two. And in a few minutes, she'd be ready to face the world again.

She was on the third deep breath and the first prayer when she heard Starr come out of her room.

Chapter Fifteen

Zach found Beau sitting at the kitchen table in the trailer he'd been assigned when he'd first hired on at the Rising Sun. His duffel was packed and waiting beside him. The trailer itself looked spotless—ready for the next man Zach hired to move right in.

"I guess I'd like my pay, sir," Beau said. "And then I'll be on my way."

Zach stared at the younger man, torn by opposing urges. He wanted to break every bone in his body for what he'd tried to do with Starr. And yet he felt sorry for him. Starr had been right. Beau hadn't had it easy. Once, his people had been proud folk. And now he was reduced to working another man's cattle to get by.

Zach remembered what he'd promised his daughter. "Starr asked me to hear what you have to say."

Beau looked right at Zach. "There's nothing. Just give me my pay and I'll go."

Zach gave it one more try. "Look. You'd better get a little honest with me here. You'd better tell me what the hell you thought you were doing with my daughter in the barn today."

Beau's jaw twitched. He looked away. "I kissed her. And unbuttoned her shirt. That's all that happened. All that ever happened."

Zach spoke with slow precision. "My daughter is sixteen."

"Yeah. I know."

"And you're what?"

"Old enough. Twenty-one."

"Then what the hell were you up to?"

Beau stared off into the middle distance. "Sometimes a guy gets hungry for more than he's ever gonna get. And then he sees something real pretty, something he knows it's wrong to take. But he's hungry. So he goes and acts like a fool. That's me. A guy who got hungry. A guy who isn't real bright."

Beau let out a long breath and turned his gaze toward Zach once more. "So, you want to beat me around a little or something?"

"Yeah," Zach said softly. "I suppose I do."

Beau got to his feet. The floor space in the trailer wasn't much, so when Beau stepped out from behind the table, he stood right in front of Zach.

"Okay," Beau said. "Do it."

Zach punched him square in the jaw, good and hard. Beau grunted and fell back against the table. Zach waited. The younger man gained his feet again and braced himself for another blow.

Zach considered, then shook his head. "That's all."

"You sure?" Beau rubbed his jaw.

Zach wasn't sure, not at all. Still, all he said was,

"Meet me by the back door of the house in ten minutes. I'll have your money in cash for you. Then you can get the hell off the Rising Sun."

Tess caught up with Starr just before she began to descend the stairs. "Starr."

The girl froze and whirled on Tess. "What?"

"Where are you going?"

"What's it to you?"

Tess looked down at Starr's feet. "Where are your shoes?"

"In my room."

"Go back and put them on. Then wash your hands and we'll go down to dinner together."

"I don't want dinner."

"Then where are you going?"

"Just mind your own business."

"You are my business."

"No, I'm not. You're no one to me." With a toss of her head, the girl started down.

Tess stood on the landing for a moment. Then, with a weary sigh, she followed Starr down.

At the foot of the stairs, Starr turned and gave Tess a fierce glare. But she didn't say anything—probably to avoid attracting the attention of everyone in the kitchen. She hurried on tiptoe out to the great room and through the entrance hall beyond. Tess followed close on her heels, closing the door behind them when they reached the front porch.

Starr whirled on Tess then, and hissed, "Stop following me!"

Tess looked at the girl levelly. "No."

Across the yard, the door to Beau's trailer opened. Zach emerged. He started down the driveway, heading for the back of the house. But when he saw them on the porch, he changed direction and strode to the foot of the front steps. "What's the matter?"

Starr leaned on the porch rail. "Daddy, what happened? Did you talk to him? Did he tell you—"

"Starr." Zach looked so weary and sad. "I thought you said you'd stay in your room."

"I couldn't. I had to know. Did he tell you how we have something special between us? Do you understand now that he never meant anything wrong to happen, that he—"

"Starr. Beau is leaving. I'm going to go get his pay and then he'll be gone."

Starr gaped at her father. "What? No. You can't do that. That's not right, not fair..." She started down the steps.

Zach blocked her path. "Go back upstairs."

"I have to talk to him."

"No, you don't. Just let the damn fool go."

"He is not a fool! He...he cares for me, that's all. He just wanted to be with me, like I want to be with him."

"Starr. Go upstairs."

She dodged to slide around Zach. He anticipated the move and stepped in her path once more, grabbing her by both arms as she ran square into his chest.

She cried, "No!" shouting now, a child denied some longed-for treasure, not caring in the least who might hear. "Let me go! Let me talk to him!"

"Starr, listen." Zach tried to hold her gently, though she kicked and squirmed and beat on his chest. "Starr. Settle down."

"No! I won't! I won't! Let me go!"

Right then, across the yard, the trailer door opened again. Beau stepped out.

Tess said, "He's coming."

Zach swore. Starr froze and glanced beyond Zach's shoulder. "Beau! Beau, he won't let me talk to you!" She tried again to break free, catching Zach off guard and almost succeeding that time. But somehow, Zach managed to catch one arm as she flew by. He hauled her back, against his chest, grabbing the other arm, too.

Beau came toward them, his stride long and swift. He stopped a few feet from where Starr stood, with her father holding her arms right behind her. Tess saw the bruise on Beau's chin—a big bruise, fresh and livid.

Starr noticed it, too. She gasped. "Beau. He *hit* you!" She shot an outraged glare over her shoulder at Zach.

Beau said, "Forget it. It's nothing."

Starr's gaze swung on Beau again. "No. He had no right to hit you! You didn't do anything. He can't—"

"Starr. He had a right."

She went still. "No!" It was a cry of pure distress. Though Tess stood on the porch, behind them all, she knew that Starr would be watching Beau's face, willing him to call her sudden, ugly doubts unfounded.

But Beau only smiled, a knowing smile. And then he actually chuckled.

"Tisdale," Zach warned in a growl.

"Zach," Tess said. "Let him tell her."

Zach turned his head and gave Tess a long, probing look. Then he released his daughter and stepped back.

Freed, Starr staggered a little, then righted herself. "Beau, please—"

Beau cut her off, his tone like a caress, "You thought you'd heard every line, didn't you, big-city girl? Heard 'em all and never fell for a one. But the lonesome cowboy routine got you goin', didn't it?"

"Wh-what are you saying?"

He made a low, smug sound. "You know damn well what I'm saying."

"No…"

"'Fraid so." Beau lowered his voice, as if sharing a secret. "Come on, you know how guys are."

Starr shook her head frantically. "No! You wouldn't. You *couldn't*. All those things you said—"

He shrugged. "They didn't mean squat. I was after one thing. And we both know what that was."

"No." The word was barely a whisper.

Beau went on smiling. "Yeah."

Zach cut in then. "Okay, enough. Go on, Tisdale. Around back. I'll get your money."

Beau turned and walked away. Starr watched him go, her face as blank as a bleached sheet.

Zach's gaze sought out Tess again, in the shadows of the porch. "Would you take her upstairs?"

Tess nodded and moved forward. Starr came to her numbly. Tess put an arm around the girl's stiff shoulders and led her toward the front door.

Inside, Edna and the others were still at the table. Tess caught sight of her friend as she passed by the arch from the central hall to the kitchen. Edna frowned. Tess shook her head.

Jobeth must have started to rise from the table, because Edna said, "Sit back down, young lady. Finish your meal."

Slowly, like very old people clinging to each other for support as they went, Tess and Starr proceeded up the stairs.

In Starr's room, Tess left the girl at the door and went to the bed. She gathered up the magazines and stacked them back on Starr's bookcase where they belonged. She set the headphones on the nightstand. Then she returned to Starr.

"Come on," Tess said, pushing the door closed and pulling Starr toward the bed. "Sit down."

The girl dropped to the edge of the bed. Tess sat beside her. They both stared toward the uncurtained windows for a time. Outside, it was still daylight, though to Tess it felt like it ought to be the middle of the night.

Starr murmured, "I'm sorry. About the curtains."

"They can be ironed again."

"I think I might have broken the curtain rod."

"It can be replaced."

"I said rotten things to you."

"Yes, you did."

"Do you hate me?"

"No. Never. That would be like…hating myself."

They'd both been sitting up as straight as soldiers. But then Starr let her head drop to Tess's shoulder. "I don't get it. You're not like me."

"Oh, yes I am. I'm a lot like you. Or I was. At one time."

They were silent again. Tess put her arm around Starr and smoothed her hair.

Starr said, "That stuff about where you and my dad sleep. That was none of my business."

"You're right. It wasn't."

"I just wanted to hurt you."

"I know. And you did. But I survived."

"I hit my dad. And kicked him."

"You behaved very badly. But it doesn't have to be the end of the world."

Starr sighed, a lonely, lost sound. "It feels like it is."

"I know. But it's not."

"I…*believed* him, believed *in* him."

"You mean Beau?" Tess felt Starr's nod against her shoulder. She stroked the black hair some more.

"I think I loved him." Starr let out another broken sigh. "I want to hate him now. But I don't. I'm just…numb."

Outside, they heard an engine start up. They both knew it would be Beau. Leaving.

After the vehicle drove off, when the sound of the engine had completely faded away, Tess asked, "Do you want to eat?"

"No. Not tonight. I'm just…so tired."

"Bed, then?"

"Yeah," Starr said. "Bed."

"Come on." Tess stood, pulled Starr to her feet and helped her get into her pajamas.

"I want to brush my teeth," Starr said, once she was all ready.

While Starr went to the hall bath she shared with Jobeth, Tess managed to hook the bent rod in place so the wrinkled curtains shut out the light.

"I really messed those up," Starr, back from the bathroom, spoke from over by the door.

Tess got down from the stool. "I'll fix them like new tomorrow." She noticed that Starr's face was scrubbed clean. "Feel better?"

"Yeah. A little."

Tess held back the covers. Starr climbed in. Tess tucked the blankets around her.

The girl sighed. "I'll say I'm sorry to my dad. Tomorrow."

"Good idea."

"Maybe it's kind of hard to believe, after today, but I really have been trying."

"We know you have."

"You'll give me another chance?"

"Absolutely."

"I'll do better."

"I believe you will."

Downstairs, Tess found Zach at the table, eating alone. Edna and Jobeth worked around him, cleaning up after the meal.

Jobeth whirled at the sound of Tess's footsteps, almost dropping the saucepan she'd been drying. "Mom. Where's Starr? Is Starr all right?"

Tess felt that all eyes were on her, waiting for her answer. "Starr is fine. A little tired."

"Will she eat?" asked Edna anxiously.

"No. She's not very hungry. She decided just to go to bed."

"Can I go up, Mom? And say good-night?"

Tess hesitated, unsure.

Zach glanced up from his dinner. "Let her go."

Tess met Zach's eyes, then turned to her daughter. "All right. Go."

Jobeth dropped the pan and the dish towel on the counter and headed for the stairs.

"Just say good-night," Tess warned. "Don't hang around."

Jobeth turned and held up a hand. "Just good-night. I promise." And she took off like a shot.

Edna turned to Tess. "Sit. I'll get you some food."

"Not much. I'm not too hungry, either."

"Some beans, a little salad. How's that?"

"That would be nice."

Jobeth kept her promise. She was back a few minutes later. She picked up the dish towel and started in where she'd left off.

Zach vanished into his office right after dinner, and later Tess heard him go outside.

Around eight, Tess walked Edna across the yard and stayed with her for a last cup of coffee. Quietly, as they sat at the table together, Tess related what had happened with Beau.

Edna shook her head. "The poor child. She acts so tough. But inside..."

"She's like all the rest of us. Looking for love."

"Maybe, after today, she'll know that love is right here. With us."

"I think she's starting to get the picture, Edna. I really do."

Tess returned to the main house at nine. She found no one downstairs, so she went up and knocked on Jobeth's door.

"Come in."

Tess pushed open the door.

Jobeth sat on her bed, wearing her pajamas, holding a black-haired doll that she'd named the Spanish Lady. The doll, dressed in red satin and black lace, was one Josh had given her not long before he died. Jobeth held up the doll. "Do you think she looks like Starr?"

Tess went and sat beside her. She smelled of toothpaste and soap. Her bangs had split in the middle, the way they always did. Tess traced the space with her forefinger.

"Mom. I asked you a question."

"Um?"

"Do you think the Spanish Lady looks like Starr?"

Tess turned her attention to the doll. "Hmm. A little, maybe. But Starr is more beautiful."

"Yes. That's true. I love Starr."

"Yes, I know you do."

"Do you love Starr?"

"I do."

"That's good. I think she'll be fine in the morning, don't you?"

"Yes, she'll be much better. In the morning. After a good night's sleep."

Jobeth slid off the bed and put the Spanish Lady back in her stand, next to four other dolls, on the bureau. "I never liked dolls that much. My real father always gave them to me. Remember?"

"Yes."

"It's hard to remember him sometimes." She straightened the skirt of a doll dressed like Scarlett O'Hara, all ready for the Wilkeses' picnic, in *Gone With The Wind.* "So it's funny, because now I'm glad to have these dolls. They help me remember him. Things like the way he would smile sometimes. And laugh."

"Yes, he had a great laugh. And a warm smile."

"Mom?"

"Yes?"

"I want to call Zach Dad. He feels like my dad. And now, after he's finished adopting me, he'll be my second dad, forever and for true, won't he?"

Tess nodded.

"Would it be all right, then? If I did?"

"It's all right with me. Maybe you ought to ask him."

"I did. I asked him first."

Tess hid her smile, thinking, Of course, she asked him first. She finds it so easy to talk to him. Easier than I find it, certainly. Easier than *she* finds it to talk to me. "What did he say?"

"He said it was fine with him, but to ask you, too."

Tess let her smile show then. "Well, all right. You've

asked him and me. And we've both said yes. So what are you going to do?''

Jobeth grinned. ''Call him Dad.''

An hour later, Tess sat in her bed with the light on, trying to read a novel that had seemed really good last night, but tonight just didn't seem to hold her attention at all.

Someone knocked at the door. She thought it would be Jobeth. Or possibly Starr.

She looked up. ''Come in.''

The handle turned and the door swung open. It was Zach.

Chapter Sixteen

Tess lowered her book and put her hand to her throat. Though she had on a plain pair of summer pajamas and the covers were pulled up to her waist, she felt totally naked.

"Is it all right if I...come in?"

Since her throat felt too tight to let words out, she nodded.

He crossed the threshold and shut the door. And then he just stood there, a tall man in a clean chambray shirt, new Wranglers and tan moccasins. For a long time, they regarded each other. His hair looked wet, as if he'd taken another shower since the one before dinner.

Her heart beat with sweet fury, to think what that might mean.

Finally he said. "I went to Starr's room. She didn't answer my knock. So I looked in. She's asleep." He smiled a little. "She looks so sweet, when she sleeps."

Her throat still felt tight, so instead of speaking, Tess nodded again.

His smile turned rueful. "Do you want me to go?"

She shook her head, vehemently.

"Then maybe you could help me out a little here."

She forced out some words. "All right."

"There. Was that so hard?"

She tugged on the covers and smoothed the sheet. "I'm nervous, I guess."

His eyes said he understood. "That's okay."

She remembered what he'd been talking about. "Starr told me she'd apologize to you in the morning."

He looked beyond her, to the windows, over which the curtains were drawn. "Do you think it's going to be okay with her?"

"Yes."

"You really mean that?"

"I do. I don't mean I think it'll be easy. But I think it's going to work out. She wants to stay with us and she's willing to change."

"What do you think about Beau?"

Tess considered, then answered, "I think life's been hard on him. And that he does care for her."

Zach made a low sound of agreement. "I think you're right."

Tess closed her book and set it on the nightstand. "I also think he's good at heart—and that he gave Starr a great gift today."

"And that was?"

"He set her free of him."

Zach pondered her words, then asked, "Did you tell her all this?"

Tess shook her head. "If she realized that he said those cruel things for her own sake, she might chase after him.

She's only sixteen, Zach. Whatever else you want to say about him and her and what's happened between them, she's just plain too young for him now.''

"I thought maybe she'd feel better, if she knew.''

"She's a proud and determined girl. And I think he's the first guy who's ever meant anything to her.''

"He is,'' Zach said. "She told me.''

"Do you think it would be the right thing, if she went running off after him?''

"Hell, no.''

"Then maybe we ought to just let it be.''

They shared another long look.

Zach said, "I always liked your eyes. Cat eyes, the way they tip up at the corners, the way they shine...''

Tess's heart beat even faster, to hear such words from him. Inside her chest there was a rising feeling. She tried to think of some appropriate reply to his compliment, but none came.

And apparently, he didn't expect a reply, because he turned away then and wandered over to her sewing area, against the wall near the big double bureau. He put his hand on her old Singer and asked without looking at her, "How long have you had this thing?''

"My parents gave it to me, as a high school graduation present.''

"That was only—what? Eight years ago?''

"That's right.''

"This machine looks a lot more than eight years old.''

"My mom bought it used. *Reconditioned,* I think they call it.''

He met her eyes at last. "Buy a new one.''

She smiled. "No. That one works just fine.''

"*I'll* buy you a new one.''

"It's the same thing, and we both know it. And the

answer is no. You've bought me too much already. Besides, I really love that old machine. And I'm used to it."

"I have not bought you too much."

She held his gaze. It felt so wonderful. Just to look at him, and have him look back. To dare to hope that his being here might mean a turning point in what they shared.

"Let's not argue about a sewing machine," she suggested in a voice that had somehow gone husky. "Or about how generous you are."

He grinned and her heart went weightless. "Then what should we argue about?"

"Nothing," she said. "Let's not argue at all."

"All right. I can deal with that."

He came closer. There was a small armchair, upholstered in maroon velvet, a few feet from the side of the bed where she lay. He dropped into it—sprawled, really, stretching his legs out and laying his arms on the armrests. For a moment, he let his head fall back and stared at the ceiling.

Then he straightened enough to look at her. She saw the heat in his eyes, as well as something else. Something that looked like resignation.

He said, in a low tone that affected all her senses, "Come here."

The breath fled her body and her mouth went as dry as a drought-stricken field.

He waited. He knew she would come. And slowly, the way a person moves in dreams, she pushed the covers away and swung her feet toward the floor.

He watched her, and the way he watched made her insides turn liquid, shimmery. Hot.

Her toes touched the small rag rug by the bedside. She could feel the pattern of the braiding all along the soles of her feet. All at once, everything, *everything* had gone so thick, so heavy—so unbearably sweet.

She stood, smiling a little, aware that the legs of her pajamas, pushed up by the covers, had dropped along her shins to their full length. She spared a moment of regret that on this night of all nights, she wore nothing more exciting than plain pink pajamas made of ordinary cotton.

She remembered the satiny nightgown and lacy negligee she had bought to wear for him. She wished she had them on right now.

But she didn't.

Some other night, she thought. And at the idea that there might be other nights, a delicious shiver went through her.

He was still waiting. She came on. His legs were open, so she stepped between them. He rested his head back again, looked at her through eyes that burned her in the most delightful way. And then he reached out. He clasped her waist. She felt the heat of his hand through the cool pink cotton.

He sat up straight and looked at her earnestly. "We got through today somehow, didn't we?"

"Yes."

"Together."

She closed her eyes for a minute, loving the sound of that word. Then she opened them. "Yes, Zach. Together."

"It's starting to seem a false thing to me, to sleep separate from you."

Her throat closed on her again when he said that, just clamped shut in pure joy. She dared to lift her hand and touch his hair. It *was* damp. And thick and silky. She felt a bright glow all through her, to think that she might begin to touch him whenever the mood struck. That they would share the closeness of two people who were truly and fully wed. She touched his jaw, found it smooth and fresh-shaven. He smelled so clean and good.

He said, "I want to stay here—in this room, in that bed—with you, tonight. Will you have me?"

She thought of the cold spring day he'd proposed to her, at that spot that she'd known must have been special to him. She remembered his bewildered look when he saw how bare it was, the way he'd remarked that it was pretty, in summer. He had asked, Will you have me as your husband, Tess?

She had answered, Yes, Zach. I will.

And then, more recently, when he said he wanted to adopt Jobeth, he'd asked, Will you allow that?

She had given him the same answer. Yes, Zach. I will.

Tonight was no different than the times before. She told him softly, "Yes, Zach. I will."

His hands moved to the bottom button of her pajama top. Trembling a little, she helped him, her own hands starting from above and moving down.

Their hands met in the middle, and she laid hers over his. Together, they parted the top, slid it off her shoulders and away. She felt his gaze on her breasts. She looked down at herself, saw the pale globes, the hard nipples. Then she looked at him again.

He whispered, "Beautiful…"

She smiled at him, still holding his hands. Gently she pressed them against her belly. They were large hands, chapped and hard-used. They covered so much of her. His fingers wrapped around the base of her rib cage. His touch felt dizzyingly rough—and so wonderfully hot. She moaned a little as the encompassing touch slid upward. For one brief, exquisite moment, he cradled her breasts.

Then his hands glided down. He took the rest of her

pajamas away, guiding them over the curve of her hips and off to the floor. She stepped back, out of them—and as she did, he rose.

Now, those burning eyes looked down at her. His broad chest confronted her. She put her hands there, against his chest, pressing a little, all at once intensely aware of the strength of him. The obdurate power.

He took her shoulders, pulled her so close. She felt her nakedness acutely, as the fabric of his shirt and jeans rubbed her tender skin. His arms went around her. She felt them, enveloping her, stealing her breath. His hands splayed at her back and her breasts pressed into his chest.

"Open your eyes."

She hadn't realized she'd closed them. But she had. She obeyed his command, raising her head fully toward his.

His mouth hovered inches from hers. She hungered for it. Longed for his kiss. And down below, she could feel him, could feel what he wanted.

The same thing she wanted: the two of them. Joined.

"Who do you see?"

She frowned, not following.

"Who? Who do you see?" He held her tighter, more urgently.

She understood then. He still thought she loved Cash. He feared she imagined doing these intimate things with another.

She caught his lip between her teeth, worried it lightly. He moaned and she knew she had his full attention. "You, Zach," she said intently, releasing the tender flesh. "Only you."

With a low, male sound, he captured her mouth. He kissed her hard and hungrily. She melted into the kiss, totally his.

His hands roamed. He found the secret place between

her thighs. She gasped, melting all the more as he caressed her there. She moved toward him, closer still, her mouth eagerly returning the demanding kiss, her body moving in welcome, encouraging his touch.

He lifted his mouth from hers, just enough to whisper raggedly, "I believe that—believe you want me." His hand continued its tormenting play below. "I believe your body is mine."

She couldn't think, couldn't answer. He lowered his head and took her breast, sucking strongly. She cried out in stunned delight as the thread of desire seemed to meet in the middle of her, stroked by both his hand and his mouth at the same time. Sensation overwhelmed her. Everything was shimmering, pulsing and contracting, then flowing outward and down in a shower of light.

Her knees buckled at the last. He scooped her up against his chest and carried her the few steps to the bed, where he laid her down.

She stared at him, as he removed his own clothes. She thought him so fine, so lean and strong. She wanted to cry and laugh at the same time.

He lay down beside her. She reached out and put her hand on his belly. It was hard and flat, with a tangle of brown hair below from which his manhood stood up proud and ready. She encircled him.

He gasped, and put his hand on her wrist, stilling any movement. "Don't. I'll lose it. I need you. Now."

He surged toward her. She fell back and he rose above her. A quick thrust, and he was inside.

He didn't move. "Stay still," he muttered between clenched teeth. A low oath escaped him.

She waited, for an eternity it seemed. Then, so carefully, she wrapped her legs around him, watching his face, seeing the intense pleasure there, and seeing pain, too, as he struggled to hold himself back.

He rested on his forearms, brought his mouth so close to hers. ''I wanted this.'' She felt his words against her lips.

''Me, too. So much.''

''And I lied.''

''No.''

''Yeah. To myself, mostly. About what I wanted from you. I wanted…everything.''

''Oh, Zach. You have it. I—''

He cut off her words with a kiss, then lifted his mouth enough to mutter, ''No more lies.''

''They aren't—''

''No. Nothing. Nothing more. Just this. Just let it be.''

She pressed her lips together. Nodded. And then moaned as he opened his mouth over hers. His tongue traced the line where her lips met. Slowly she opened for him, allowing him in, kissing him fully, letting him taste her, tasting him back.

Then, as he kissed her, he began to move.

She gasped and then sighed. They shared the same breath, in the kiss that went on and on, as he moved inside her, slowly, deliberately, making her feel every stroke. She thought she would pass out, from the sheer glory of it. Her whole being rose toward him, moved away, beckoned him back once more. She felt that she surrounded him, and yet was within him at the same time.

The rhythm grew wilder, rougher, harder. She clutched him tight, pushed herself up toward him.

And in the end, they found the peak together. She felt him stiffen, heard his guttural cry just as her body bloomed into a completion of its own.

* * *

She must have slept for a time. When she woke, the room was dark. She could feel the warmth of him, smell the scent of him. He was here at last, beside her in this bed, where she'd almost stopped dreaming he would ever come to claim her.

She thought he was sleeping. But then he touched her, his hand curving on her breast, trailing down over her belly, unerring, relentless. He found the female heart of her. She was ready for him, her legs falling open, her whole body so eager she gave not even token resistance.

He stroked her, slowly, touching everything, missing nothing. She moaned and moved at the command of his caresses. She cried his name. And tried to say her love.

But he wouldn't allow that. His hand stopped its play to move up and close over her mouth. She smelled her own desire, felt its wetness on his fingers.

"No," he said.

She nodded, like a captive sworn to silence on pain of torture or death. And shameless, she lifted herself toward him. He gave her what she sought, resuming the loveplay, finally entering her again when both of them were crazy with the scent and feel of each other.

It was frantic, needful. It went on and on.

Later, she woke again. Felt the slight soreness from the times before. Still, she couldn't stop herself. She reached for him once more.

Chapter Seventeen

When Zach woke beside his wife the next morning, the room lay in darkness. Slowly Zach turned his head to look at her.

She lay on her back. He studied her profile. She was smiling. Her arm was thrown back on the pillow by her head, the pale skin giving off a pearly glow in the darkness, her fingers loose and slightly open. He couldn't repress a smile. She looked relaxed. Content. She took up a good portion of the bed, too. Under the covers, her legs were wide apart. That amused him. She was such a tidy woman, and yet she slept in an abandoned sprawl.

He thought of the night before.

And wanted to reach for her, wanted to hear her welcoming sigh, feel her move toward him, twining her legs with his, eager and hungry for his touch.

But he didn't.

He belonged to her now. He understood that. That was

just the way he was. He'd held out as long as he could. But when he gave his body, he gave his heart.

A glance at the clock on the nightstand told him that it was near six. Beyond the heavy drawn curtains, dawn would be breaking. They should have been up and around an hour ago, but neither of them had given much thought to setting the alarm the night before.

He considered the morning chores he always took care of before breakfast and decided that Tim could do them.

Zach needed some time. He needed a long ride on Ladybird, out somewhere he wouldn't see another soul. He needed time to accept what he understood now, to make his peace with it, and to clear his mind. Then he would feel up to handling the rest of the day. Up to dealing with Starr. Up to deciding whether to take Cash's suggestion and put together a little range patrol of his own.

Up to facing his wife and telling her honestly that he loved her with all of his heart and he would do his best to get past the fact that she didn't love him.

He thought of that place he'd taken her, in the spring, when he'd asked her to marry him. Now, the cottonwoods would have their leaves and the grass would be green. It was as good a destination as any—and fitting, in a way.

He slid from the bed with great care, sure he was going to wake her. But she only sighed and flung her other arm out, commandeering what was left of the bed.

Quiet as a thief, he crept around to where he'd dropped his clothes. Swiftly he scooped them up and pulled them on. Finally he tiptoed out, closing the door so carefully behind him that he managed to keep the latch from clicking when it caught.

He stopped in his room to put on a pair of socks. Then he went downstairs, where he found Jobeth at the table drinking hot chocolate and Edna bustling around the kitchen.

"We wondered if you would *ever* get up," Jobeth groused.

Edna asked anxiously, "Is Tess all right? She never sleeps this late."

He made his tone offhand. "She's fine. A little tired. We forgot to set the alarm. I thought I'd let her catch a few extra winks."

"Good idea." Edna attacked a big bowl of pancake batter with a wooden spoon. "I'll have this breakfast on in two shakes, just you watch."

"Great." He almost turned for the door where he'd left his muddy boots the afternoon before. They'd be dry now, and fine for a ride in any case. But then he decided he'd better say something to Edna about where he was headed. He'd get her all stirred up if he just rode off without a word. "Listen. I'm going out riding. For an hour or two."

Jobeth jumped up. "I'll come."

He gave her a smile. "No, I need your help here."

Her face fell when he said no, but brightened at the news that she could help him. "Anything. Sure."

"I haven't done my chores yet. I wonder if—"

"Yeah. I can do them. I can handle that."

"You get Tim. He'll help."

"Sure. All right. I will. I'll get going right now—Dad." Her face turned the cutest shade of pink.

He couldn't hold back a grin. "Thanks." She was out the door almost before he got the single word out of his mouth. He heard her whistle for Reggie when she got to the back step, and a glance out the kitchen window showed the child and the dog racing for the barn.

He could feel Edna's gaze on him. He faced her.

"When Tess wakes up, tell her not to worry. I'll be a few hours, no more."

"Where are you going?"

"Northwest. A little place I know along the creek, out near the Farley breaks."

"Are you…all right, truly, Zach? You seem—"

"I'm fine. And I'll be back soon."

"You *will* catch those cattle thieves. And Starr *will* be okay."

"I know you're right—at least about Starr. And don't worry." He grinned at her. "Get those pancakes on. Lolly and Tim are probably starving."

"Go on. Let me do my work." She made a shooing motion, then turned back to the counter and her breakfast preparations.

Zach stepped out to the back porch, shucked off his moccasins, pulled on his boots and went out the way Jobeth had gone. Within ten minutes, as dawn began to bleed the night from the sky, he was mounted on Ladybird and headed toward the Big Horns that towered so jagged and uncompromising on the western horizon.

Tess woke smiling—until she opened her eyes and found herself alone.

She sat up. "Zach?"

And then she looked at the clock. She blinked. Looked again. "Six-thirty!" she exclaimed aloud, imagining everyone down in the kitchen, seated around an empty table, wondering if breakfast would ever be served. She threw back the covers and jumped from the bed.

She'd just emerged from a two-minute shower, yanked on some clothes and raked a comb through her hair when someone knocked at the bedroom door.

She blushed crimson and grinned like a fool as an image of Zach flashed through her mind—Zach carrying a breakfast tray, all loaded up with two eggs, bacon, toast, a steaming cup of coffee—and maybe even a bud vase containing a single red rose.

Where he'd get the rose was a mystery, of course, since she hadn't got around to planting any yet. But maybe a wild rose. She'd seen a few, out near the creek. Now that would be something. Breakfast served to her on a tray, and a wild rose in a bud vase, brought to her by her husband, who ordered her back to bed where he would sit next to her adoringly as she ate.

Oh, she had to stop this foolishness. Any ranch wife who expected breakfast in bed either had a broken leg or an unclear understanding of her own responsibilities.

There was a second knock. Tess smoothed her hair and went to the door.

It was Starr, dressed in jeans and a clean T-shirt, her face scrubbed free of makeup, though the rhinestone still glittered in her nose. For some reason, Tess found the sight of the sparkly stone reassuring.

Starr said, "Edna told me not to bother you, but I thought I heard the shower going and I—"

Tess took her arm. "Come in." She pulled the girl into the room and shut the door. "How are you?"

"Okay. I was looking for Dad, but Edna said he was gone."

Tess waved a hand, dismissing that idea. "He's probably out in the barn. I...think he might have gotten a late start on his morning chores."

"Edna said he was having Jobeth and Tim handle his chores."

Tess frowned. "Why?"

"Edna said he went riding, about twenty minutes ago. That he'd be back in a few hours."

Tess made a low sound of disbelief. "A three-hour ride. By himself. That will take up half the morning." In summer, mornings were prime working hours. A lot could be accomplished before the heat of the day made tough jobs all the harder.

Starr said, "Edna told me he just wanted a little time to himself." She moved a few steps away, then turned back. "But I know what that means. It means he's trying to decide what to do with me, after what happened yesterday."

"Starr." Tess put on a stern expression. "Stop this."

Starr threw up her hands. "I feel like such a...nothing. All dirty and awful inside, you know?"

Tess reached out, put her arm around the girl. "Listen. Yes, your dad *is* worried about you. But there's more going on. Yesterday, he and Jobeth found more tire tracks."

"The rustlers?"

"I'm afraid so. He's worried about that—and a few other things, I suppose."

"What things?"

"Not-your-problem things."

Starr let out a groan, then grew earnest. "So then, what you're saying is, if he's really bugged, it's not only about me?"

"Exactly."

"And he didn't talk to you about anything like, um, sending me away?"

"Starr. Listen. No one is sending you away. No one wants you to leave. Unless you go back with your mother—"

"Never. Please. Don't make me go back there."

"We won't. Not if you don't want to."

"You promise?"

"I promise. Will you believe me?"

"All right."

"So. If your mother's not an option—"

"She's not."

"—then you belong here with us. We will insist that you stay at least until you're out of high school. And after that, you'll always have a place here, though by then the choice to stay or not will be your own."

Starr gnawed on her lower lip. "You mean that, don't you?"

"I do."

The girl let out a long breath. "Well. Okay."

Tess gave Starr's shoulder one last squeeze. "Now. I suppose Edna is getting the breakfast?"

"Yeah."

Just then, the bell started clanging outside.

Tess said, "Come on, then. Let's go down."

"I told that girl to let you sleep," Edna said when Tess and Starr got to the kitchen.

Starr jumped to her own defense. "She was up already, I swear."

"Well, all right then. It's just as well, I suppose. The food's on the table and ready to eat. Starr, pour the milk for you and Jobeth. And how about coffee, for the rest of us?"

"Sure." Starr went to work.

Tess hovered in the arch from the hall, thinking about Zach, feeling a growing unease. "Edna, where did Zach say he was going?"

"Some place along the creek, Northwest, out by the Farley breaks."

Tess knew the geography of the Rising Sun well

enough now to be reasonably certain that was the place he'd taken her the day he proposed.

She recalled the night before, a pleasant weakness washing through her at the sweet memory. And she thought of his words to her.

I lied, he had whispered, To myself, mostly. About what I wanted from you. I wanted....everything.

She had tried to tell him that he *had* everything. Twice, she had tried to tell him—three times, if she included that night out by the horse pasture when they'd talked about Starr. But he wouldn't hear her.

He wanted her love. And he had her love.

But he wouldn't let her say it.

Because he thought it was a lie.

Now he'd gone and run off to sit by the creek and feel sorry for himself. Worrying everyone. Because he wouldn't see the truth when it bit him on the nose.

Lolly, Tim and Jobeth came trooping in.

"Sit down, sit down," said Edna. "And you, too, Tess. Come on now, the food will get cold."

Tess took her seat. The business of serving and passing dishes began. She helped herself to the food and passed the platters as they came by her.

But her mind remained on Zach.

Okay, she could understand why he didn't believe her. Her love was no real prize, to be fair. She had thought she loved Josh once, as a foolish girl of seventeen. And then she'd been so sure she would love Cash forever.

And now, those other loves were as nothing. Like lightning bugs in a long-ago night—next to her love for Zach, which shone as bright as the sun.

Oh, she shouldn't have let her body rule her last night. She should have pushed him away, ordered him to sit there in that maroon velvet chair, until she told him that he was the only one for her. Over and over, she should have told him. Until he finally got so sick of hearing it that he gave in and believed her.

But she hadn't. She had wanted him too much. She'd been afraid that if she tried to force him to hear her out, he might turn and leave her, as he had done so many nights before.

So she had kept quiet. And he had stayed. They'd shared a beautiful night.

And now, come morning, he was out there by the creek somewhere.

Feeling sorry for himself.

It had to stop, that was all. It had to stop now. Today.

"Tess, you haven't touched a bite."

She stood. "Edna, can you handle things here?"

"What now?"

"I'm going for a ride."

Halfway to his destination, Zach let himself through the gate into a pasture where he and his men had put several Hereford cows and their calves, along with a few registered Black Angus bulls. He closed the gate and then remounted, clicking his tongue at Ladybird, who started up a rise a hundred yards from the gate. Zach let the horse have her head as she carried him up to the crest. His eyes were on the clean morning sky, on the mountains and on the striated ridges of the breaks that became clearer up ahead as he topped the rise.

His mind was on Tess. Which was why he let himself get in plain sight of the sweep of land below him before he really registered what he saw there: a pickup and stock trailer, two men and a dog.

Chapter Eighteen

The men below had a set of portable panels in place and it looked like the dog had already bullied a couple of cows and their calves up the ramp.

Where the hell was that cell phone when he needed it?

Swearing under his breath, Zach sawed on the reins and turned back—hoping to hell that he hadn't been spotted.

Once over the rise again, he slid off of Ladybird, pulling his rifle from its saddle scabbard, scanning the landscape for cover that would take him closer to the men below.

But he was too late. Just as his boots hit the ground, Beau Tisdale stood from behind a boulder ten feet to his left, a little below the crest of the rise. He held a .30-30 just like Zach's own.

Unfortunately Zach's rifle was pointing at the ground. Beau had his pointed straight at Zach.

"Throw it down," Beau said.

Carefully, Zach knelt and set his rifle on the ground.

Keeping Zach firmly in his sights, Beau commanded, "Move back, away from the weapon."

Zach did as he was told.

"Now go on." Beau gestured with the rifle barrel. "That way, back over the rise."

By then, Zach had got a good look at Beau. The younger man was a hell of a sight. His left eye was an ugly purple and swollen nearly shut. He had welts along his jaw, a mean-looking goose egg standing out from his right cheekbone and a lot more bruises than the one Zach had put on his chin. "What happened to you?"

"I ran into a door. Now, move."

Cautiously Zach backed up the rise. Still pointing the rifle at him, Beau slid between him, Ladybird and the .30-30 he'd thrown down. Zach reached the crest. His hands in the air, he stood silhouetted against the sky. The men below must have seen him then. He heard them shout.

"Turn around," Beau said. "And head on down."

Zach was putting it together. It all seemed so clear now. "Your brothers are down there, right? And you've been the spy for them, relaying which stock is where—and which pastures to keep clear of because we'd be working them."

Beau said nothing. He just kept that rifle trained on Zach's chest and his finger on the trigger. A gun went off, down below. The shot went nowhere, but Zach ducked beneath the crest again anyway.

Beau swore under his breath. Keeping his rifle trained on Zach, he stalked up the rise. At the top, he shouted down, "I've got him! Stop shooting, dammit!" He spoke to Zach. "Come on. Move."

Zach held his ground and spoke gently. "They beat holy hell out of you, because you messed up their gravy train, didn't they? Getting mixed up with my Starr like that, getting stupid. Getting caught.'' Zach looked right in Beau's eyes over the barrel of that .30-30. ''I bet there are Montana plates on that pickup. And your brothers got themselves a deal with some sleazeball in a packing plant over the state line.''

''Move.''

''This is bad business, Beau. You know it. That's why you didn't stop me before I hit the top of that rise and saw what was going on down below. You didn't stop me until I got off my horse. If I'd just ridden away, you would have let me go.''

''I told you to move.''

''Come on, Beau. You know it's over now.'' He took a step toward the younger man.

''Stop. Freeze.''

''Give me the gun, Beau.''

''Just don't, Mr. Bravo. Don't come closer. I'll shoot.''

In the distance, over the rise, Zach could hear the other men yelling. They'd have started clawing their way up now, unable to drive the pickup and half-loaded stock trailer at such an angle, and having no horses to ride.

He had a minute or two, max. To talk Beau around to his side. Or to take him. Or to get himself shot.

Zach took another step. And another.

Beau said, ''Damn your eyes.'' And pulled the trigger.

The shot exploded into the morning stillness. When the sound faded off, Zach was still standing. ''Missed me. On purpose, I'd say.''

Beau ejected the spent shell and chambered another. ''Stop.''

And Zach pounced. Beau grunted at the impact. The rifle exploded a second time, the sound so loud, it might have been the end of the world. Zach felt the bullet sizzle along his side.

Ignoring the stinging pain over his ribs, he concentrated on dealing with Beau, on getting both hands on the weapon and trying to wrestle it free. They rolled several yards with the rifle between them, off the crest and down the side Zach had come up. They'd both lost their hats by then. They rolled right over one of them.

When they stopped, Beau was on top. He pulled back and yanked the rifle away. Zach held on. Beau let go of one end and tried to land a punch. Zach blocked it with the stock of the weapon. Beau yelped with pain as his fist connected with wood. They rolled some more.

As they struggled, Zach could hear a dog barking, coming closer. And not far away, Ladybird snorted and pranced, not liking this one bit more than Zach did.

And then, at last, things started to go Zach's way. He got a firm hold on both the pistol grip and the barrel. He had himself on top. He rocked back onto his knees, then gained his feet in a crouch.

The rifle tore free of Beau's grip. Beau grunted and stared at Zach, stunned. For a split second, Zach thought he had things under control.

Then Beau's eyes shifted, widening, looking beyond Zach's shoulder. Zach didn't even have time to turn before something exploded against the side of his head. The world went blindingly bright—and then narrowed down to a point.

And then faded away to nothing at all.

Sometime later, Zach came swimming up to a semblance of consciousness. He didn't feel so great. His head throbbed and his stomach roiled. His side still burned.

"You tie him up good, boy?" That would probably be J.T., the oldest of the three Tisdale boys.

"I did." Beau's voice. "Good and tight. He's goin' nowhere till we figure out where we want to take him."

Zach kept his head down and his body loose. He must have made no sound as he came to, because they talked as if he were still out cold.

"Okay, let's finish up here." J.T. again. "He's dead to the world and goin' nowhere. You get back up on lookout, Beau."

Zach heard footsteps turning, loping away.

"Don't you let us down again!" A third man's voice— had to be Lyle Tisdale—commanded.

No answer from Beau.

"You hear me, boy?" Lyle shouted again.

After a moment, Beau called back, "I heard!"

"Let's go," J.T. said.

Zach heard other boots moving away. A whistle. Cattle lowing, a dog barking. Hoofs pounding a ramp. Somewhere not too far away, a horse snorted and shifted. That would be Ladybird.

Zach identified the object at his back. A tire and wheel. It felt like Beau had tied him to the pickup wheel.

Carefully, making a supreme effort not to show movement, he tested the ropes that held him. He felt a little bit of play.

Maybe Beau was thinking about changing sides in this game.

Damn, his head felt like a split-open watermelon. A wave of dizziness came washing over him....

Riding the gray mare, Tess topped the rise from which the Farley breaks started to show up pretty clear.

She saw what was going on down there—including Ladybird, tied to the front bumper of the pickup, and what had to be Zach, bound to the rear wheel.

She reached for her Colt.

"Hands up, Mrs. Bravo," said a voice from behind and slightly to her right.

She turned enough to see the owner of the voice—and the rifle he had aimed at her.

She shook her head. "Oh, Beau. What are you up to now?"

"Throw down that pistol, Mrs. Bravo. Real careful-like. And then slide off that mare, slow and easy."

He must have passed out again, briefly, because Zach found all of a sudden that he was awake again. He heard more shuffling of hoofs, and an endgate being lowered and hooked. He stayed limp, head hanging, though his hands were already working at the knots that bound him.

A man whistled and the cab door of the pickup opened, several feet to his right, on the opposite side. He knew then that he'd been tied to the rear wheel, on the driver's side.

"Get on in there, Queenie," J.T. said. The pickup rocked a little as the dog jumped in the cab. The door was slammed shut.

From a few feet away, Lyle let out a shout. "Whooee! Look who Beau's caught now."

"Aw hell," J.T. said. "Just what we need. The little woman."

Tess staggered down the pasture side of the rise. Beau followed behind her, leading her mare, carrying his rifle over his shoulder and using her own Colt to keep her in line. The closer she got to the pickup and the man tied against the rear wheel, the less she liked what she saw.

She walked faster, wanting to get to him, wanting to prove to herself that he was all right. He had to be all right....

As the ground leveled out a little, she broke into a run, her hat blowing off her head and bouncing against her shoulder blades. Nobody did anything to stop her—probably because she was headed right where they wanted her.

One of the two men by the truck made a few rude, whooping sounds. Tess ignored him. She ran straight for the limp figure tied against the wheel.

"Zach, oh Zach..." She dropped down beside him, wrapped her arms around him. "What did they do to you? Oh, Zach. You wake up, now. *Please,* open your eyes. I mean it, Zach Bravo. Open your eyes right this instant!"

She felt so warm. Her neck was moist with sweat. She held him so tight, smashing his nose against the leather thong that held her hat on. It was so fierce and hungry, the way her arms clutched him. Her voice trembled in fear at the same time as she commanded, "Open your eyes right this instant!"

She sounded so frantic. She sounded like she might just go crazy if she lost him. She sounded like...

A woman in love.

Like a light going on inside his head, brighter than the sun, brighter than a thousand suns, the truth came to him: Tess loved him.

Dammit.

She loved him.

He had what he wanted from her. He had everything. He had it all.

But not for long, if he didn't get them out of this.

She stroked his head, letting out a small cry of dismay

when she felt the hard lump where he'd been hit, pulling his face so close into the crook of her neck that he dared to whisper, "Be ready."

She stiffened, just a little. But she was a crackerjack in a crisis. He would swear the Tisdale boys didn't have a clue what she'd heard.

She started in on those Tisdales. "What is the matter with you? He needs a doctor, can't you see that? You untie him this instant. You get us straight into town."

J.T. started laughing. "A doctor? You think we'll take him to a doctor? That's a hundred-dollar hoot."

Lyle started cackling away, too. Only Beau was silent.

Then J.T. got serious. "All right. Listen up. We gotta get the hell out of here. What do we do with them?"

"Er, shoot 'em?" Lyle suggested helpfully.

Zach worked at the rope. It wouldn't be long now....

Tess held Zach's head lightly. She had heard and understood his message. She tried to look like nothing more than a distraught wife, while she used her body to shield his movements as he worked at his bonds.

"Do murder?" Even with his face all battered, Tess could see Beau grow pale. "Not that. Come on, J.T. Not that."

J.T. scratched his bearded chin with the pistol he carried. "Well, now. We can't just let 'em go. They've seen us."

"We got no choice, the way I see it," said the third man. "We gotta get rid of them for good and all."

"Lyle, no," said Beau. "Not murder. Murder's no good."

"Don't talk back to your elders," Lyle snarled.

Tess felt the slightest brush of Zach's hand against her

back. He had done it! Somehow, he had worked his hands free. The moment to act would be coming up fast.

Hope and fear making her heart beat so loud it seemed as if she could hear nothing else, Tess glanced at their captors, one by one, assessing the possibilities for over-powering them. Beau had both her Colt and the rifle he'd drawn on her, one in either hand. At the moment, both of those weapons were pointed at the ground. J.T. had that pistol. The third man, Lyle, wasn't armed.

Tess knew that Zach always carried a rifle when he rode out alone, one similar to Beau's. But she didn't see it anywhere close.

"I know," J.T. said. "There's that old homesteader's cabin, out near the breaks. We'll take the two of them there, tie them up inside, and set fire to the place."

"Good idea," said Lyle.

"We'll start a damn grass fire," Beau argued.

J.T. shrugged. "A big fire wouldn't be half-bad. Wipe out any evidence good and proper."

"What about the horses?" Beau sounded desperate.

J.T. looked at him as if he had no brains at all. "We'll turn 'em loose. They'll wander home. So what?"

"Someone will find our tracks here. And with two people dead, they'll put a lot more effort into figuring out what the hell's happened than they have been so far."

"We'll be long gone, boy. Over the state line. The cattle will be hanging in a meat locker. And we'll take the pickup and trailer apart for junk." J.T. gestured with his pistol. "So come on." He gave the gray mare a slap on the flank that sent her galloping off. "Give Lyle all the hardware and tie up the woman. We gotta get gone."

Beau didn't move.

J.T.'s lips drew back from his yellowed teeth. "*Now,* boy. Like I said."

Beau stayed unmoving for a split second more. Then he said one word, "Tess," and tossed her the Colt.

Everything went crazy. From beside her, Zach erupted into action, pouncing on Lyle. J.T. fired his pistol, catching Beau in the thigh. Beau cried out, but not before he fired the rifle. J.T. went down, and fired again, hitting Beau in the shoulder. Somehow, Beau stayed on his feet. He aimed slow and steady at J.T.

J.T. tossed his pistol away and shouted, "Don't shoot, you little bastard! Can't you see I'm hit?"

Through the exchange of gunfire, Zach, his legs still tied, rolled around on the ground with Lyle.

Tess rose slowly. She pointed the Colt at her husband and the other man and commanded, "Zach, get me a clear shot."

Obediently he rolled beneath his adversary. She stepped up and put the Colt to the back of Lyle's head.

"Don't move," she said gently. "Don't even breathe."

Chapter Nineteen

As soon as Zach was on his feet, Beau handed him the rifle. Zach gave it to Tess to hold, along with J.T.'s pistol, which she stuck in her hip holster. She felt like a regular human arsenal.

Next, Zach ordered the Tisdales into the back of the pickup. They had some trouble getting the two injured men in there, but Beau and Zach managed it, with Tess keeping her Colt trained on the whole operation. After that, Zach tied up Lyle and J.T., though J.T. moaned and complained the whole time about how hurt he was.

"We have to take you in, too," Zach said, when he came to Beau.

"I know it."

"You need to be tied?"

"No, I do not."

"You're dead, boy, when I get my hands on you," Lyle muttered to Beau.

Zach said, "Shut up."

Lyle started to say something else, but Zach clipped him a good one on the jaw. Lyle was quiet after that.

Zach turned to Tess. "Keep watch on them. I'll get the cattle out of the trailer."

"Fine."

Tess stood guard as Zach bullied the cows and their calves out into the sunlight. Next, he unhitched the trailer and hobbled the horses. Then Zach jumped in the back of the pickup with the Tisdales.

"You drive. To the sheriff's office in Buffalo," he said to Tess.

She handed him Beau's rifle. Then, when she opened the driver's door, she saw Zach's rifle in the gun rack.

"Zach. They put your rifle right up here."

"Trade me," he said.

She took his rifle down and gave it to him, then put Beau's rifle in the gun rack. The whole time, the stock dog watched her from the passenger side of the seat, friendly and panting, as if he hadn't a clue they'd just tied up his masters.

Finally she drove them all to the sheriff's office in Buffalo, with the dog sitting happy as you please on the seat beside her.

Later, after Lyle had been booked and Beau and J.T. had been taken to the hospital under armed guard, Zach and Tess gave their statements and turned the dog and the Tisdales' weapons over to a deputy. They both made a point to speak kindly of Beau, to explain how he had come over to their side in the end. The arresting officer said Beau's change of heart would be considered, but there was probably no way he'd avoid doing time.

It was near noon before they were done answering all the questions. They used the phone at the station to call the Rising Sun. Edna answered, and Tess told her an abbreviated version of the morning's events.

"Oh, my sweet Lord. Are you both all right?"

Tess looked at her husband, who stood right beside her. "Zach's got a bullet graze, along his ribs. And one heck of knot on the back of his head. But he's still standing. And still ornery. The doctor patched him up, but I can't get him to stay in the hospital."

"That man," said Edna. Tess knew she was shaking her head. "Well, then. You come on home now."

"Can't. Not yet. A deputy's driving us back to the pasture where it happened."

"Whatever for?"

"He wants to look over the scene. Plus, we left the horses there. And Zach lost his hat. He wants to look for it. "

"And *then* you'll come home?"

Zach took the phone from Tess. "Look, Edna. Could you handle things there for a little more. Please." She must have said she would, because Zach grinned at the phone. "We'll be home for dinner. That's a promise."

Tess grabbed the phone again. "Give the girls our love."

"Well, certainly. I'll do that. I think I'll make Swiss Steak. How does that sound?"

"Delicious. Put those little bits of green pepper in it, like you always do. And not too heavy on the onions."

"Yes, I did go a little overboard on onions last time. I'll go lighter with them today."

Zach took the receiver for the last time. "Edna. We really have to go now."

Tess could hear her, giving one last bit of unheeded advice, as Zach hung up the phone.

* * *

The horses were there, nibbling the grass, pretty much where they'd left them. And they found Zach's hat, smashed flat, right where he'd lost it, on the far side of the rise. Zach beat it against his thigh to loosen it, then reshaped the creases as best he could.

"Good as new," he declared.

Tess refrained from comment.

The deputy looked around and took pictures of the scene before he left. As soon as he'd driven off, Tess took two aspirin from the first-aid kit in her saddlebag and passed them to Zach, along with her canteen.

He looked down at the little white pills in his hand, then up at her. "Always ready with whatever I need." He tossed the pills into his mouth and washed them down with a long drink from the canteen.

She watched him. "I really don't like the look of that goose egg you've got."

"Let it be," he muttered gruffly, settling his battered hat more firmly on his head.

"And I'll bet your side hurts like the devil. I think I should—"

"Stop fussing." He capped her canteen and handed it back. She hooked it in place.

They mounted the horses. And then, as one, they turned for that spot under the cottonwoods where Zach had asked her to marry him back at the end of April.

With the trees in full leaf, the spot was shaded now. Cottonwood fluff blew around in the air. The boulder that Tess had found so cold to sit on was warm and dappled with sun. She perched on it again, folding her hands in her lap, feeling almost as nervous as she had on that cold spring day two months before.

Zach cleared his throat. "Tess, I..."

She looked up at him, thinking of all the things she herself had to say, not knowing how to begin.

He said, "I guess I love you."

The words didn't surprise her, but they did fill her with joy. She looked down at her hands, swallowed and looked up at him once more. "And *I* guess I know that now. Since last night. Since…the way it was. And what you said, about wanting it all."

He had more to say. "I think I might have loved you almost the first time I saw you, hiding behind the punch bowl, the day Cash married Abby."

Her heart skipped a beat, and then started pounding faster than before. "You loved me since *then?*"

He nodded. He had to cough again. "But I didn't let myself admit it. I saw what a good wife you'd make. And I focused on that. I think I knew all along about your feelings for Cash."

"You did?"

"Yeah. But I didn't let myself see it. Not until after I'd asked you to be my wife. By then, I could tell myself it was too late to back out. That you were too perfect for my needs. That since it would be a practical arrangement, it didn't matter what you felt in your heart."

She dared to whisper, huskily, "But it did matter."

He looked off, toward the mountains. "Yeah. It did. I guess that, in the end, what goes on between a man and a woman can never be entirely…convenient."

"No, Zach. I suppose that it can't." She looked down at her folded hands, torn between joy that he truly did love her—and fear that he would never believe she loved him as well.

He confessed, "I rode off by myself today to…get myself straight with all of this. When I came back, I was going to tell you that I would try to live with loving you, even though you didn't love me. Because you and me together, well, it works so damn well. Don't you think?''

''Yes, Zach. It does.''

He scooped off his hat and dropped it in the grass. ''A hard day seems half the effort it used to be, since you became my wife. You finish what I start, you know what to do before I even have to tell you. And to have you in my house, filling it with your smiles and your laughter, with your caring ways—that's everything to me. But a man's heart is a headstrong thing, Tess. And I was having trouble. I couldn't help wanting you to feel for me what I feel for you.''

Tears pooled in her eyes. She didn't know where they came from. She really was a woman who had been done with tears long ago. Dashing the moisture away, she nodded. ''I do understand, Zach. And I'd...I'd like to say a few things myself now, please. If you'll hear me.''

He looked at her for a long moment, then replied, ''All right. Say your piece.''

She gulped, brushed at her eyes again and began. She told him of the wild-hearted seventeen-year-old she had been. How what she'd thought was love for Josh De-Marley had quickly faded to grim duty. And she told him what he already knew—of the hundred ways Cash had come to her rescue, through all the tough times.

She said, ''I honestly believed I loved your cousin. For years. Lately it's occurred to me that believing I loved Cash was a way to keep love alive in me. A way to keep hoping, when there wasn't much left to hope for. A way to keep something shining and fresh inside me, when what I really felt was just plain used up and helpless—barely in my twenties, with a hopeless wandering dreamer for a husband, a little girl to raise, and no chance to advance myself on any job I did manage to get.''

She rose from the boulder, took off her own hat and tossed it in the grass beside his. Then she looked up intently into his beloved, craggy face. "Oh, but, Zach, now, with you, I've learned what real love is. Because I've found it at last. And it's so much deeper and finer a thing than I ever knew. It's…having so much in common, wanting the same things. And yet still feeling that little catch of excitement, feeling my heart beat faster from a look or a smile. It's…it's you, Zach. You are my love."

She thought for a moment that she saw tears in his eyes, too. And then he turned away.

She looked down at her boots, at their hats so close together, at the shiny green grass. "I knew you wouldn't believe me. Why *should* you believe me? I haven't been honest, ever, I know it. I don't think I ever really loved Josh. And the love I felt for Cash was nothing more than gratitude, in the end. Why should you think I even know how to love?"

"Tess."

She forced herself to meet his eyes again. And she gasped. His sun-lined face looked so young, suddenly. And full of joy. He took both her hands. "I do believe you."

She stared at him. "You do? But how can you?"

"I felt it in the way you held me. I heard it. In your voice."

"But I don't understand. You mean last night, that you knew last night?"

"No, for some reason, I couldn't see it then. It wasn't till a few hours ago, when you found me tied to that pickup wheel, when you jumped on me and grabbed me and ordered me to open my eyes."

"A few hours ago?"

"Yeah."

She felt more than a little bit irritated with him. "You knew, you *believed,* when we got here, to the creek? You knew I loved you *then?*"

He released her hands and backed up a step. "Now, Tess. Don't go getting yourself worked up."

"But, Zach. You didn't tell me. You let me say...all those embarrassing things...."

"You asked to talk before I was finished." That mouth she loved curled in a sheepish smile. "And besides..."

She looked at him sideways. "Besides, what?"

"I guess I wanted to hear what you said. It was beautiful, what you said. And the part about me, about how I'm so special to you, how we think alike and want the same things. How you get excited when you see me. That was real...edifying."

"You liked it."

"Yeah. I did."

"It was...edifying?"

"Yeah, I believe that would be the right word."

They stared at each other. And then they were smiling at each other. They started to laugh—and then, all at once, Tess found she was crying.

He reached for her, pulled her close. "Hey. It's all right. It's good. You know it is."

She buried her face in his shirt. "I...I've been so ashamed."

He stroked her back. It felt like heaven, to have him hold her this way, to have him show her such tender care. "You've been on your own," he murmured, "struggling to make a life with some dignity in it. You've done your best."

"I've lied in my heart."

"Tess Bravo, you don't have to lie anymore."

She looked up at him, swiping at the darn tears. "That's good. I'm glad of that."

His gaze strayed to her mouth. "Kiss me, Tess."

And she did, there in the shadows of the cottonwood trees, with the creek rushing past a few feet away and the warm summer wind sighing all around them.

Not too much later they mounted up for the ride back. Zach gave her a smile. "Ready?"

She nodded, her heart so full, thinking how beautiful and impossible life could be. Eight years ago, she had foolishly left the ranch she loved. She hadn't known then that she would never return.

And yet, in her heart now, she felt just as if she had found her way back.

With her true love at her side, Tess Bravo turned her horse for home.

*   *   *   *   *

Coming in October of '98, meet Billy Jones, the newest member of Christine Rimmer's beloved Jones Gang. Enjoy a sneak preview of this emotion-packed Silhouette single title release!

Billy Jones turned off the Jeep, silencing a great Randy Travis tune in mid-note. Then, for a moment, he sat studying the two-story building where Prue had brought his son to live.

He estimated the place to be anywhere from forty to a hundred years old. It had been freshly painted white, with the trim and shutters a dark green. It had a nice, deep porch and a white picket fence around the yard. A big old rough-barked locust tree hung over the fence, looking a little scraggly now that it was losing its leaves for the winter. But the lawn was thick and green and the slate walk that led up to the porch steps seemed to just invite a man to come inside.

He had to admit it. The place seemed like just what Prue had been looking for—the perfect setting for Jesse to get a good start in his "ordinary" life. It was also across and down from the white frame community church.

Leave it to Prue, he thought with some amusement, to find a house on the same street as the church.

Billy got out of the Jeep and went around back for his garment bag, suitcase and guitar. He slung the bag over his shoulder and took the suitcase and the Martin in either hand. Then he went through the front gate and up the pretty slate walk.

The look of stunned disbelief on Prue's face when she opened the door made the trip more than worthwhile. Now all he had to do was find that meddling uncle of his and knock his teeth down his throat. Then Billy Jones would be a totally contended man.

"Billy." She said his name the way some might say, "measles," or "poison oak." Her glasses had a smudge on them. She wore jeans and an old shirt and her hair had a red bandanna over it.

"Getting a little cleaning done?"

"Billy," she said again, dazed. Disbelieving.

He savored her obvious stupefaction at the sight of him, here, where she had been so sure he would never come. "Your mouth's hanging open, Prue."

She snapped it shut.

"Can I come in?"

She fell back, still wearing an expression of pure befuddlement. Feeling really good, really happy, really pleased with himself, Billy entered her house. It had no entry hall, so he stepped into her living room. It was just what he had expected—hardwood floors and comfortable furniture, roses floating in a cut crystal bowl on the coffee table. The television was new, with decent-size screen, but there was no stereo in sight. He'd have to do something about that.

He set the guitar and the suitcase down, though he kept the garment bag on his shoulder. "Where's Jesse?"

"Taking a nap."

He grinned. "In a bed, I hope."

She frowned. "He's too young for a bed."

He put on a reproachful expression. "He's still in a crib?"

"Uh, yes. Yes, he is."

"Well, I'll have to fix that." He grinned again. Ever since she'd left him in his office that night a week ago, he'd been making plans. For the things that he would fix.

Behind the smudged glasses, her eyes had lost that dazed look. They were starting to glitter dangerously. "Wait a minute. How dare you assume you can just march in here and—"

He cut in, sounding very reasonable, he thought. "He sure does sleep a lot. That worries me a little."

"He's hardly more than a baby. Babies do sleep a lot."

"Still, it could be a warning."

"A warning of what?"

He had no idea, but he wasn't going to tell her that. "Hell, lots of things."

She folded her arms under her breasts and tapped an impatient foot on the floor. "Oh, right. You're an expert on children now. After all, your experience with them is so *vast.*"

She was starting to irritate him. "When it comes to my son, my experience is going to get *vaster,* Prue. Just watch." He hoisted the Martin and the suitcase again. "Now, where's my room?"

She blinked at him through those grotesque glasses, which he knew damn well she wore as much to hide behind as to see through. "Your room?"

He hefted the suitcase, just in case she hadn't noticed it. "I'm staying a while. Contrary to your expectations, I'm taking you up on that offer of yours."

"What offer?"

With relish, he reminded her, "You know, to visit? To get to know my son. To learn how to be a father."

"But, you can't—"

"Oh, yes, I can." He stepped a little closer to her. "Unless...."

She moved back. "What?"

"...you were lying to me."

She gulped. "Lying?"

"About how I was so welcome to come and stay. Any time. Were you lying about that, Prue?"

Her eyes darted back and forth, as she desperately tried to find some avenue of escape. But there was no escape, and Billy knew it. He'd done a lot of thinking about Prue. And he'd come to a few conclusions.

The woman was hopelessly honorable. And she possessed an ingrained determination to do the right thing. Honor and integrity. Such commendable qualities. Qualities that put her right where he wanted her....

* * * * *

*The surprises are just beginning. More Joneses
are coming in the fall of '98....*